"There is no death here . . ."

Over fifty million Americans
believe they have had encounters
with persons who have died.
(National Opinion Research Center)

Now comes evidence from
the other side:
Authenticated cases of people
brought back from clinical death
who describe going out-of-
body to comfort distant loved ones.

Kathrine Egan, while pronounced
dead, made final contact with
her mother . . . 2,000 miles away!

Marc Levin accurately described
"seeing" his wife in the
waiting room while his own body
lay dead on the operating table!

How does science explain?

DEATH ENCOUNTERS

BY CHARLES FIORE
AND ALAN LANDSBURG

DEATH ENCOUNTERS
A Bantam Book / July 1979

ISBN 0–553–12432–8

Published simultaneously in the United States and Canada

Bantam Books are published by Bantam Books, Inc. Its trade-
mark, consisting of the words "Bantam Books" and the por-
trayal of a bantam, is Registered in U.S. Patent and Trademark
Office and in other countries. Marca Registrada. Bantam
Books, Inc., 666 Fifth Avenue, New York, New York 10019.

PRINTED IN THE UNITED STATES OF AMERICA

Contents

Introduction

Four Kinds of Survival Evidence

On the morning of April 12, 1975, Martha Egan prepared breakfast for her husband and daughter in their split-level home near Boise, Idaho. Between mixing a pitcher of orange juice and tending the bacon, she scanned the list of things she would do that day. First was a call to her mother, in Vermont, who still had not recovered from a bout of winter flu.

This morning Martha did not feel well. She had awakened with a tight sensation in her chest—a sore muscle or congestion? she had wondered—and now she noticed that her breathing was shallow and labored. The constriction worsened and soon was accompanied by a numbness in her lips. Shortly after her family sat down to breakfast, Martha Egan suffered her first heart attack.

As the ambulance pulled into the emergency entrance of the local hospital, Mrs. Egan suddenly stopped breathing. The attending medic could detect no pulse: clinically, Martha Egan was dead. A team of doctors and nurses beat on her chest and forced oxygen into her lungs. Though she was unquestionably unconscious—in fact, "dead"—Martha Egan witnessed the entire resuscitation procedure from a vantage point outside her body. But her story is very different from the tales told by most people who have been revived from clinical death.

She was not concerned with the possibility that the resuscitation efforts might fail. Instead, she worried about how her ailing mother might take the news of her death. Martha later recalled:

"If I was going to die, I felt that I had to be the one to tell Mom the bad news. I had to assure her that I didn't mind dying if I had to, that being dead wasn't bad. Actually, it seemed very pleasant."

No sooner had Martha thought about contacting her mother than she saw an image of her sitting in a chair beside her bed in her home in Vermont.

"Mom was reading in her favorite chair. I was still in the hospital emergency room, yet at the same time I was also in Mom's bedroom. It was amazing, being in two different places—and so far apart—but space seemed like a meaningless concept. I said, 'Mom, I've had a heart attack and I might die, but I don't want you to worry. I don't mind dying if that's what I must do.' But she didn't look up.

"I went closer to her chair and sat on the edge of the bed. I was just a few inches away from her. She seemed absorbed in her book, I may have glanced at the title, but I can't recall what it was. I only know that somehow I had to get her attention. I was afraid to touch her for fear that I'd scare her to death. 'Mom,' I kept whispering, 'it's Martha. I have to talk to you.' I was trying to think of another way to get her attention when suddenly my focus was back in the emergency room. I was back in my body."

Martha Egan began breathing on her own and her heartbeat returned to normal, but she remained unconscious until about eleven o'clock that night. She awakened to find her husband and daughter beside her bed, and her brother who lived in Connecticut with them. That night, she assumed that her husband had called her family and her brother had flown to Idaho. But a few days later she learned something different. Her brother had indeed received a call at his New York law office, but it had come from their mother. She had had a strange feeling that something had happened to Martha and insisted that her son investigate. After several phone calls he learned the truth, and caught the first flight to Idaho. Had Martha Egan really traveled out of her body across two-thirds of the United States and contacted her mother?

Martha feels that she did just that. Her mother, who died last year, could only say that she sensed that something was wrong but had no idea what it was or how the fact had dawned on her.

Martha Egan's story is rare but not unique. Many people revived from clinical death report that they tried to contact a loved one during their out-of-body experience (OBE). Most, however, are not successful. But those who are "sensed," "heard," or on rare occasions even "seen," by living human beings are opening up an entire new area of research into survival of bodily death and the existence of an afterlife. What is sensed, heard, or seen? An astral body (the etheric double of the physical body)? If so, can its presence be detected with sensitive scientific equipment? By studying different kinds of death encounters, scientists are devising new ways to investigate the possibility that the dead can contact the living. Martha Egan's case offers one kind of evidence for survival, and, as we shall see, suggests one scientific line of investigation. The case of Marc Levin, an engineer in Grand Rapids, Michigan, suggests another.

Marc spent most of his out-of-body (OB) time

trying to get the attention of his wife, Peggy, who was seated in the waiting room two floors below the operating theater where Marc had "died" during emergency heart surgery. He recalled:

"It was the most frustrating experience of my life. I could see Peg as plain as day sitting there wringing her hands in her lap, looking very worried. She was frightened but I wasn't and I wanted to get this across to her."

Marc tried to talk to Peggy but soon realized that his voice rang only in his own ears. Then he resorted to other tactics:

"I touched her gently. I didn't want to scare her. But she didn't seem to feel my hand on her arm. Then I tapped harder and harder. Finally I tried taking her hand in mine and lifting it—I couldn't. Peggy was aware of none of this. There was an empty vase on the table next to her and I thought, That doesn't look too heavy—maybe I can knock it over to get her attention Well, I tried several times, pushing and pulling the damn thing, trying to get it rocking so at least she might hear the noise."

There are some obvious similarities between the stories of Martha Egan and Marc Levin, and one major difference: at a subliminal level, Martha somehow was able to contact her mother and convey to her a "sense" of trouble, while Marc Levin could in no way contact his wife. Yet, Marc correctly perceived that his wife was waiting in a blue-and-white tiled room two floors beneath the operating theater, and later he gave a fairly accurate description of the clothing she had worn that day.

For purposes of scientific analysis, the two cases should fall into two distinct categories. Unfortunately,

4

it has become a common practice among researchers to lump all types of death encounters into one class of evidence for survival. Some people who have life-threatening experiences never try to contact a loved one. Others leave their body but travel no farther than the ceiling of the emergency room; occasionally they can later produce facts that prove they witnessed their own resuscitation while unconscious. Still other people become totally absorbed in a surreal, spiritual experience while they are clinically dead. They see brilliant lights, hear celestial music, drift through dark voids, and meet spirits of deceased relatives and friends. On awakening, they often recount tales of great mystery and beauty; but tales cannot be scientifically substantiated. Thus, death encounters run the gamut from ineffable personal experiences to cases at the other extreme where the "dead" contact the living. To facilitate the scientific study of life after death, we propose that death encounters be divided into four categories: Death Encounters of the First, Second, Third, and Fourth Kind. This numerical terminology is frequently used in physics, mathematics, chemistry—and more recently in UFOlogy—to distinguish levels of significance of various phenomena. Death encounters have various levels of significance, and it seems auspicious to recognize this fact. In this book we will examine death encounters based on the following definitions:

Death Encounters of the First Kind: This classification includes people who, while clinically dead, unconscious, or in a severe life-threatening situation, have an out-of-body experience (OBE) but later can provide *no factual evidence* to support their encounter. It remains purely a subjective experience. Most of the cases collected by Dr. Raymond Moody and Dr. Elizabeth Kubler-Ross are of this nature. Death Encounters of the First Kind are often studied collectively to determine common elements that lend credibility to individuals' tales and suggest that they might represent a universal human experience at the time of death.

Death Encounters of the Second Kind: This category includes people who can give factual evidence, such as bits of conversation among medics in the emergency room, a physical description of the equipment used to resuscitate them, or an accurate account of events that took place at a distance while they were unconscious. The case of Marc Levin is a Death Encounter of the Second Kind. Such encounters have objective components and consequently are suited for study by the scientific method.

Death Encounters of the Third Kind: This category includes clinically dead or unconscious people who convey to another person what we might call a "gut feeling" concerning their condition. This is the first instance where "contact"—perhaps by some form of ESP—is made between the "dead" and the living. Death is broadcast, so to speak, and certain people, usually those with close emotional ties, pick up the message. The person whose life is threatened does not have to travel astrally, but the message of danger can be conveyed telepathically. The distinguishing characteristic of this classification is that the recipient of the message generally has only a vague idea that something is wrong with someone with whom they are acquainted. Usually they do not know who the person is or what the life-threatening situation is about. In this sense, the full message of danger may be received at a subliminal level of the mind, but only part of it—the sensation of uneasiness it engenders—surfaces to conscious awareness. At other times the death message can be clearer. The recipient, however, *never feels* the contact. The case of Martha Egan and her mother is one example of a Death Encounter of the Third Kind.

Death Encounters of the Fourth Kind: Such cases involve direct parasensory contact between a living person and one who is either permanently dead, clinically dead, unconscious, or in a severe life-threatening situation. The person who is out of his body is "seen," "heard," or detected in some parasensory way. The recipient *is aware* that he or she is in paranormal contact with a a spirit or an astral being. This is the most impressive evidence for survival, and the phenomena popularly known as "taped voices from the dead" and "spirit photography" (which are dealt with in a later chapter) fall into this category.

This book is not meant to be a comprehensive study of these categories; rather, it presents a pioneering look into four kinds of death encounters and what each suggests about survival. It offers a new approach, one that we believe could yield fruitful results.

The book is divided into three parts. Part I contains cases of the four kinds of death encounters, backed by recent scientific findings that support the paranormal aspects of each case. In Part II we examine some of the thorniest problems confronting today's doctors and theologians: When is a person really dead? In their haste to preserve usable organs, do doctors sometimes unknowingly "kill" a patient who they believe is dead but who could in fact be resuscitated? Might that person be having an OBE and be conscious of what is being done to him? Why do we fear death? Are OBEs really minideaths, rehearsals for the final flight? And finally, what can we learn from Eastern cultures about dying a peaceful death and about an afterlife? After examining the latest evidence on survival, in Part III we turn our attention to the scientists who are simulating death in the laboratory and trying to detect the spirit that departs the body—and trace its flight. Finally, we consider the issue of "life before life." For, if the spirit survives bodily death, reincarnation is not unlikely. We will see that by searching out the traumas, misfortunes, and misbehavior of "past lives," many people today are being cured of neuroses and even some physical ailments.

Death was openly discussed in Western countries a century ago, but sex was taboo. Today, the roles are reversed; sex is a common topic of conversation, while death has for many years been almost unmentionable in polite society. Now there are signs that the taboo on death is dying. With it comes renewed interest in the questions "Is there life after life?" and "Was there life before life?" Recently, Andrew M. Greeley, director of the National Opinion Research Center of the University of Chicago, and a Roman Catholic priest, headed a vast poll to determine how Americans feel about death. He came up with a surprising statistic: twenty-seven percent of the American population—or fifty million people—feel that at some time they have been in touch with someone who has died. "Belief in contact with the dead," says Greeley, "is widespread. Over fifty million people have had such experiences; six million have had them often."

Greeley also found that women are far more likely than men to have contact with the dead. And those women who have lost a spouse are the most likely to have such experiences. A simple debunking argument, of course, is that such experiences are purely exercises in imagination, by which a lonely wife tries to avoid the harsh reality of death. "But," says Greeley, "it could also be argued that if somehow the barrier that separates the living from the dead can be penetrated, it would most likely be accomplished precisely by those who are still united in a powerful bond of love. Who else, in other words, would be expected to maintain contact after death?" Greeley concludes his highly respectable study with these words: "It is astonishing, perhaps a little unnerving, to know that more than one-quarter of the American people have had contact 'several times' with the dead.''

The most familiar ancient account of a person returning from the dead is the biblical story of Lazarus, the brother of Mary and Martha and friend of Jesus. Unfortunately, the Gospel of John does not tell us what Lazarus experienced during the several days that he was dead, but philosopher L. N. Andrieve wrote: "For three days he had been dead. Thrice had the sun risen and set, but he had been dead; children had played, streams had murmured over pebbles, the wayfarer had stirred up the hot dust in the highroad but he had been dead. And now he was among them; he touched them, he looked at them, and through the black discs of his pupils, as through darkened glass, stared the unknowable beyond." Lazarus's lips remained sealed about his experience, but today many Americans are freely talking about their own encounters with death. Theologians are listening raptly to these tales, philosophers and scholars are drawing striking parallels between the stories of twentieth-century Americans and the ancient writings of Eastern mystics, and an increasing number of scientists are actually attempting to duplicate death in the laboratory so that they might be able to trace the flight of the spirit, or soul, or astral body, to its next resting place.

In this book we will carefully examine the most recent evidence available that suggests the existence of an afterlife, and that under appropriate conditions it is possible to have communications between this life and the next one.

PART I

1
Death Encounters of the First Kind

Death Encounters of the First Kind are the ones most often studied because they are the most frequently reported. Thousands of people annually are revived from clinical death or survive near-death accidents, and it is estimated that about fifteen percent of them have stories to tell. Their highly subjective nature makes them the least convincing in terms of "hard" proof that the spirit can survive bodily death; yet, analyzed collectively, their many common elements cannot be ignored. Before we can appreciate death encounters of higher orders, it is essential to understand what is known about the first kind of evidence for survival.

Not everyone who has a brush with death reports exactly the same kind of experience. But Iris Zelman, a thirty-six-year-old grammar-school teacher in Flint, Michigan, had a typical Death Encounter of the First Kind.

"I was in the intensive-care unit following open heart surgery for the replacement of a valve. Suddenly I felt a sharp pain in my chest. I screamed and two nurses soon were wheeling me back to the operating room. I felt the doctors attaching wires to my chest and an injection in one arm. Then I heard one of the doctors say, 'We've lost her.'

"I noticed that a white mist, like fog, surrounded my body and was drifting toward the ceiling. At first I was mesmerized by the mist, then I realized that I was looking down on my body and my eyes were closed. I kept saying to myself, 'How can I be dead? I'm still conscious!' The doctors had cut open my chest and were working on my heart.

"The blood made me squeamish and I looked away, sort of upward, and realized that I was at the entrance of what seemed to be a long, black tunnel. I've always been afraid of dark places, yet I entered this tunnel. Immediately I was traveling toward a white light far ahead and heard eerie but pleasant sounds. I had an irresistible urge to become one with the light.

"Then I thought of my husband, and I felt sorry for him. He's always been so dependent on me for everything. He couldn't live without me. At that moment I knew that I could either continue toward the light and die, or return to my body. Spirits surrounded me, figures I couldn't identify . . . I stopped traveling. I was definitely depressed that I had to go back for my husband's sake—I felt obliged to—when suddenly a voice, unlike anything I've ever heard, very authoritative yet gentle, said, 'You have made a good choice and you will not regret it. One day you will return.' I opened my eyes and was looking up at the doctors."

No element of Iris Zelman's experience can be scientifically verified. It remains a highly personal encounter. Chicago psychiatrist Dr. Elizabeth Kubler-Ross, who has been counseling dying patients for over two decades, believes that stories such as Iris Zelman's are not hallucinations. "Before I started working with the dying, I did not believe in a life after death," said Dr. Kubler-Ross. "Now I believe in one beyond a shadow of a doubt."

One of the things that has convinced Dr. Kubler-Ross—and an increasing number of scientists—is the common elements found in thousands of death encounters related by people of vastly different ages, cultures, races, and religions. Some of the most common elements culled by Dr. Kubler-Ross and by Dr. Raymond Moody in his study of over two hundred death encounters are:

Peace and Contentment. Many people describe extremely pleasant feelings and sensations during the early stages of their experience. After a severe head injury one man's vital signs were undetectable. He later said: "At the point of injury there was a momentary flash of pain, but then all the pain vanished. I had the feeling of floating out of my body in dark space."

A woman who was resuscitated after a heart attack remarked: "I began to experience the most wonderful feelings. I couldn't feel a thing in the world except peace, comfort, ease—just quietness; I felt that all my troubles were gone."

Ineffability. People who have close encounters find their experience ineffable, or difficult to describe in words. Iris Zelman reported, "You really have to be there to know what it's like." Another woman put it this way: "The light was so dazzling that I can't really explain it. It's not only beyond our comprehension, but beyond our vocabulary."

Psychologist Lawrence LeShan, who has studied psychics and mystics for their experiences of "cosmic consciousness," feels that ineffability comes not only from the extreme beauty of a transcendent encounter, but primarily because all such experiences transcend our four-dimensional, space-time reality and therefore transcend logic—and language evolved strictly from logic. Raymond Moody, in *Life After Life,* gave this example of a woman who "died" and was resuscitated. She said:

"Now there is a real problem for me as I'm trying to tell you this experience, because all the words I know are three-dimensional. What I mean is that when I was taking geometry, they always told me there were only three dimensions [ot space], and I always just accepted that. But they were wrong. There are more. . . . Of course, our world—the one we're living in now— is three-dimensional, but the next one definitely isn't. And that's why it's so hard to tell you this. I have to describe it to you in words that are three-dimensional . . . I can't give you a complete picture of it verbally."

Noise. One man who "died" for twenty minutes during abdominal surgery described "a painful buzzing in my ears; then it sort of hypnotized me and I was peaceful." A woman heard a "loud ringing, like chimes." And others have heard "celestial bells," "heavenly music," "whistling sounds like the wind," and "the rhythm of ocean waves." Virtually everyone who has stared death in the face has heard some repetitive sound.

No one is absolutely sure what these sounds mean, but ironically—or coincidently, however you wish to look at it—such sounds are mentioned in the ancient *Tibetan Book of the Dead,* a work compiled around 800 A.D., which we shall examine in a later chapter. Briefly, the book details the stages of death. According to the text, at one point after the soul has left the body, the person may hear alarming sounds that might frighten him, or pleasant sounds that lull and soothe him. Scientists are amazed by the number of predictions made about the dying experience in the Tibetan text that also appear in stories of twentieth-century Americans who have had a death encounter and have never read the Tibetan book.

Seeing Spirits. Edward Megeheim, a fifty-six-year-old professor who "died" on an operating table during cancer surgery, claims he met his deceased mother. "She spoke to me. Told me I had to go back for now. I know it sounds crazy, but her voice had a reality to it that has stayed with me to this day." Peter Tompkins, a student who "died" twice, first in a car accident and later during chest surgery, met deceased relatives on both trips beyond.

Seeing spirits is not the most common feature of death encounters, but it does occur. Dr. Karlis Osis, director of the American Society for Psychical Research, in New York City, found a greater frequency of this phenomenon in his studies of dying patients in the United States and in India. Dr. Osis refers to the apparitions as "take away" figures—deceased relatives or friends whom the patient feels have come to escort him out of this world. The Reverend Billy Graham calls them angels.

Many skeptics have argued that such figures are merely figments of a dying person's imagination, conjured up to comfort them in making the transition from life to death. In Freudian terms they would be called wish-fulfillment figures. But Dr. Osis strongly disagrees: "If the take-away figures were merely wish-fulfillment, we would find that they would come more often to patients who were expecting to die, and less often to those who thought they would recover. But there is in fact no such relationship."

The Light. Variously described as "brilliant," "dazzling," and "blinding," yet never hurting the eyes, light is one of the most common elements of death encounters, and the one with the most direct religious symbolism. According to the studies of Raymond Moody, "Despite the light's many unusual manifestations, not one person I interviewed expressed any doubt whatsoever that it was a being, a being made of pure light." Many people have described the light as a very personal being with a definite personality. "The love and warmth which emanate from this being to the dying person are utterly beyond words," said Moody. "He feels completely surrounded by it, taken up in it; he belongs to it and is part of it."

For singer Carol Burlage, who "died" while giving birth to her second child, the light had a voice. "Suddenly it spoke to me. It told me I must go back, that I had a new baby who needed me. I didn't want to return, but the light was very persuasive." She said its tone was neither male nor female but neuter; Iris Zelman and many others agree. "Since my experience," says Carol, "I'm constantly reminded of Jesus's words, 'I am the light.'"

Dr. Pascal Kaplan, dean of the School of General Studies at John F. Kennedy University, in Orinda, California, and an authority on Eastern religions, noted that the light reported by dying individuals is also mentioned in the *Tibetan Book of the Dead*. "It plays a central role in all Eastern religions," Dr. Kaplan said. "The light is seen as wisdom or enlightenment and as such it is the ultimate goal of the mystic."

Dark Void or Tunnel. This seems to be a transition from one level of reality to another. Many people claim that they instinctively felt that they had to cross through the blackness before they could attain the light, which invariably is located at the remote end of a tunnel. "The void is not frightening," reported Iris Zelman. "It is the only expanse of blackness that I have ever found inviting, almost cleansing." Another woman described the tunnel as an "echo chamber where every word I spoke rang in my head." In all cases, penetrating the blackness is, symbolically at least, a rebirth experience.

Out of the Body (OB). Almost without exception, all people who report death encounters of any kind experience liberation from their physical bodies. Their perspective can be shifted to virtually any location in space, proximate or remote, and they can travel great physical distances in a flash, merely by thinking of the place where they want to be. As we will see later, many researchers believe that OBEs, which can be induced by simple relaxation techniques, are actually minideaths, or rehearsals for the final step. There is strong evidence to suggest that having an OBE can remove the fear of death and make the process of dying easier and more pleasant.

Sense of Responsibility. Many people say they "came back" because they felt that their work on earth was incomplete. Duty made them choose to return. Singer Peggy Lee was appearing at a supper club in New York City in 1961 when she collapsed backstage. She was rushed to the hospital with pneumonia and pleurisy. Her heart stopped and for about thirty seconds she was clinically dead. Peggy Lee had a very pleasant OBE, but she experienced great torment over whether to return. "The pain would be a small price to pay to live for the people I loved," she later recalled. "I couldn't stand the sadness and frustration of leaving my daughter." Martha Egan's sense of responsibility was to her mother. Iris Zelman's was to her husband. We will see that it is this sense of responsibility that most often results in cases of contact with the dead or the dying—or Death Encounters of the Fourth Kind.

The onset of clinical death is rapid. It is triggered by such things as a heart attack or a severe shock to the brain or nervous system, or it is the consequence of a violent accident. Whatever the cause, the effect is an abrupt transition from life to death. Collecting and analyzing reports of people revived from clinical death is, in a way, peeking at death through the back door—the reports come only after stepping over the threshold and returning. But what do people experience just before they die a normal, gradual death, when they approach death through the front door? If the sounds and imagery of death that we have just discussed are genuine, universal phenomena, then they should be the same no matter which way death is approached.

Drs. Karlis Osis and Erlendur Haraldsson tackled this question in a recently published four-year study of fifty thousand terminally ill patients in the United States and in India. The two psychologists wanted to know exactly what a patient sees and hears just moments before he dies. For the most part, they believe, these would be subjective experiences, or Death Encounters of the First Kind. However, with the help of hundreds of doctors and nurses who had worked directly with dying patients and had been present at the moment of death, Osis and Haraldsson came to some startling conclusions.

We know that suffering often precedes dying. Cancer spreads rapidly through the body and brings torture in its final stages, pain that sometimes cannot be alleviated even by drugs. Severe heart attacks bring intense pain radiating from the chest to the arms. Patients terminally injured in accidents suffer the agony of fractured bones, contusions, and burns. Yet Drs. Osis and Haraldsson found that just moments before a natural death, suffering is replaced by calmness. As Dr. Osis told us, "Patients seem to light up in expressions of harmony and serenity." A ten-year-old boy suffering from cancer suddenly sat up in his bed, opened his eyes wide, and smiled for the first time in months, exclaiming in his last breath, "Mother, it's beautiful!" He then fell back onto his pillow, dead.

Cases vary widely in richness of communication just before death. A nurse in a large hospital in New Delhi reported the following:

"A female patient in her forties, who was suffering from cancer and during the last days had been depressed and drowsy, though always clear, suddenly looked very happy. A joyful expression remained on her face until she died five minutes later."

Often a patient does not utter a word, but his or her facial expression can be reminiscent of a description of ecstasy in religious literature. Unexplainable physical changes can also occur; this happened in a case in the United States, which a nurse reported:

"A woman in her seventies, suffering from pneumonia, was a semi-invalid who spent a painful, miserable existence. Her face became so serene, as if she had seen something beautiful. There was a transfixed illumination on her face—a smile beyond description. Her features were almost beautiful on so old a face. Also, her skin had a transparent, waxy quality—almost snow-white— so different from the usual yellow discoloration that follows death."

The nurse who observed this patient felt that the woman might have had a vision that "just transformed her entire being." This serenity lasted until her death an hour later. How does one account for the old woman's suddenly lambent, youthful skin? One faith healer who has worked with terminally ill patients claims that near the time of death she often sees an aura of light surrounding the patient's body. "The glow transforms the skin and hair as though it were an infusion of pure energy from some external source," she said. Laboratory evidence, which we will examine later, clearly demonstrates that light phenomena are also associated with voluntarily induced OBEs. Researchers now believe that the energy that comprises the astral body is radiant light energy—a claim that psychics and mystics have made for centuries.

Sometimes the change that overcomes a patient is otherwordly not only to physics but to everyone near-by. One hospital spokesman reported this about a fifty-nine-year-old woman who suffered from pneumonia and cardiac ailments:

> "The expression on her face was beautiful; her attitude seemed to have changed entirely. This was more than a change of mood. . . . It seemed as if there was something just a little beyond us that was not natural. . . . There was something which made us feel that she was seeing something that we did not see."

What magnificent visions do the dying see? How do months or years of pain suddenly vanish? Dr. Osis suspects that the mind "loosens up," becomes less tightly connected with the body, when a person is near death. The astral body is preparing to separate from the physical body, and as death approaches, the physical body and all its woes become less significant.

Following is a typical case where pain and misery suddenly disappeared. The physician who reported it was the director of a city hospital in India.

> "A male patient in his seventies had been suffering from advanced cancer. He had been in great pain and was sleepless and restless. One day after he had managed to get a little sleep, he woke up smiling, seemed suddenly free from all physical pain and agony, detached, calm, and peaceful. For the last six hours the patient had received only a very moderate dose of phenobarbital, a relatively weak sedative. He bade all good-bye, one by

one, which he had not done before, and told us that he was going to die. He was fully alert for some ten minutes. Then he fell into a coma and died peacefully a few minutes later."

According to traditional religious beliefs, the "soul" leaves the body at the time of death. Psychics say that the soul and the astral body are the same thing. According to Dr. Osis, apparently whatever leaves the body can do so very gradually. "While still functioning normally," says Dr. Osis, "a dying patient's consciousness, or soul, might be gradually disengaging itself from the ailing body. If so, we could expect awareness of bodily sensations to gradually decrease."

Some patients speak before they die and many of these insist that they have glimpsed persons long dead, scenes of otherworldly beauty, and much of the same imagery reported by people who have been revived from clinical death. In one American study, more than two-thirds of the dying patients saw apparitions that "called," "beckoned," and sometimes "demanded" that the sick person come to them. One doctor reported that a sixty-year-old woman suffering from intestinal cancer suddenly sat up in bed and called to her deceased husband. "Guy, I'm coming," then smiled peacefully and died.

Could these voices, images, and lights be nothing more than hallucinations caused by illness, by drugs, or by deterioration of the brain? We know that high fever, medication, uremic poisoning, and brain damage can cause some very convincing hallucinations. Researchers have found that the most consistently logical, detailed stories are told by the patients who are the healthiest up until the time of death. "The sick-brain hypothesis does not explain the visions," concludes Dr. Osis. "It looks like patterns are emerging consistent with survival after death."

If a person can glimpse the hereafter before he dies,

might he be able to give some factual evidence to substantiate his vision? In other words, can a normal death produce an Encounter of the Second, Third, or Fourth Kind, as clinical death sometimes can? Such instances are rare, but researchers have found cases that offer confirmation. For example, one doctor reported this about a hospitalized woman who was about to die.

"She told me she saw my grandfather beside me and told me to go home at once. I went home at four-thirty and was told that he had passed away at four. No one had expected that he would die at the time. This patient had actually met my grandfather."

The changes that take place near the moment of death often mystify doctors. It seems that even patients with severe mental or emotional problems become remarkably lucid and rational just before death. Dr. Kubler-Ross has observed this in a number of her chronic schizophrenic patients. This fits well with the conclusion that near the time of death, the astral body (consciousness or soul) is gradually separating from the physical body. This is further reinforced by a case in which a doctor reported that a twenty-two-year-old man who had been blind all his life, suddenly, in the minutes before his death, glanced around the room, smiling, apparently seeing doctors, nurses, and, for the first time, members of his family.

It cannot be mere coincidence that both clinically dead patients and hospitalized patients who die slowly report a hereafter peopled with spirits of the deceased, a land of great serenity and peace that fills the person with a fervent wish to attain it. Thus, the experiences of the dying, no matter how they approach death, are fundamentally the same, and they seem to make sense only when we assume that something about the human body survives death.

The concept of an afterlife exists in all cultures, and each has its own images of heaven and hell. If a collective picture could be culled from an examination of various cultures and ethnic groups, how would it compare with the reports of today's dying patients?

In the Christian tradition, heaven is a hierarchical state in which angels and saints enjoy the presence of God and contemplate His being. The Koran promises the faithful a paradise strictly reflecting male Arab tastes; it has the form of a beautiful oasis with gardens, rivers, and luscious trees, and men are clad in silken robes and lie on couches feasting on fruit and wine. Less hedonistic, classical Greeks believed in a beautiful island located over the waters of the Atlantic at the world's end. It had a perfect climate, with no rain, snow, or strong wind, and its fertile land bore honey-sweet fruit year round. Orphic mystics envisioned heaven as a joyful resting place for pure spirits, located under ground.

The Aztecs distinguished three different paradises to which souls went after death. The first and lowest, Tlalocan (land of water and mist), was a place of abundance, blessedness, and serenity, where the dead sang, played leapfrog, and chased butterflies. The trees were laden with fruit and the land was covered with vegetables and flowers. The second heaven was the land of the fleshless; it was an abode for those who had learned to live outside their physical bodies and were unattached to them. The highest paradise was the House of the Sun, a place for those who had achieved full illumination. They were the privileged ones, who were chosen as daily companions of the sun and lived a life of pure delight.

In the Nordic tradition, access to Valhalla was gained on the basis of martial prowess; there, warriors engaged in splendid tournaments during the day and at night feasted on pork and meat. In Hinduism, the re-

gions above the clouds are places of beauty and joy
and are inhabited by deities. To the North American
Indian tribes, the deceased inhabit the region of sun-
set, or the "happy hunting grounds." Eskimos see their
dead in the radiance of the aurora borealis, joyfully
playing with the head of a walrus. Thus, we see that the
concepts of heaven are diverse, and the physical characteristics are undoubtedly expressions of the desires of
the worshipers. The same diversity is true for the various concepts of hell.

If these beliefs are based on facts, shouldn't resuscitated modern-day Catholics, to take one group as an
example, report seeing the traditional elements of the
hereafter that they learned from an early age? One
would suspect this to be the case. Yet, among all the
reported experiences of dying, virtually no Catholics
have claimed to see St. Peter standing at the Pearly
Gates, or Christ seated at the right hand of God, or
choirs of angels. In fact, a statistically insignificant number of people have reported seeing the "standard"
imagery of heaven as it is described by their own religion. One possible explanation is that the hereafter does
indeed exist but does not conform to the descriptions
given in any of the sacred books of any of the major religions. Another possibility is that clinical death with
its accompanying imagery is only the first, and the
most fundamental, step toward the place commonly
called heaven. Indeed, it would be presumptuous to
assume that what is briefly glimpsed at the threshold of
death, or during clinical death, is the hereafter in all its
infinite detail and grandeur.

Even a glimpse of another eixistence would be comforting to many people. It is one thing to accept a belief on faith and quite another to experience it first-
hand. Thirty-six-year-old Richard Coleman, an electri-
cian who had a ten-minute brush with death during
lung surgery, said that people often ask him whether

there is any experience in life that can give us a clue to what clinical death is like. "What they really want to know," he reported, "is if there is some situation they can safely experience that will give them even a vague idea of what it feels like to die." While most psychical researchers would say that an OBE might be the answer, since it involves separation from the physical body, Coleman feels that dreaming is the experience that most closely resembles death.

There is considerable historical weight for that answer since Western philosophers as far back as Plato believed that there existed a common element between death and dreaming. What might it be like to be conscious without a body? Plato asked. What would one be conscious of? Where would one's consciousness reside? How might different people recognize one another? How would they communicate?

Philosopher H. H. Price, in his major paper "Survival and the Idea of 'Another World,'" has theorized that postmortem perceptions will be similar to dreams and that they will be formed from mental images acquired during one's lifetime. In other words, everything we experience in this life—the beautiful and the horrible, the good and the bad—forms a repository of the things we can experience in the next life. He further theorizes that the laws of the postmortem world will not be those of physics (which govern the material world) but of psychology, since our survival will be psychological.

Whereas our dreams are private experiences in which other people appear only as our visions and not as independent entities in their own right, in the hereafter, Price believes our visions will be as real as ourselves— and spirits will communicate via telepathy and other forms of ESP. This telepathic activity will produce visual and auditory images, and the resulting experience will be just like that of seeing and hearing other people.

The next world will be fashioned by the power of

our desires, Price feels, but he cautions us against assuming that such a realm would be uniformly pleasant, for our dreams reveal with unerring accuracy the real character of our desires, including those that are repressed during our waking hours. They might well be hellish dreams rather than heavenly ones. In Price's view, our dreams give us a glimpse of the nature of the hereafter—an idea that stems from early tribal beliefs.

Whether there is any fact in the dream-death hypothesis, it does pose an important question—one too often overlooked by thanatologists, who collect tales of death and dying. In any study of the encounters of clinical-death victims, we must remember that some—albeit a very small percentage—experience hellish visions. The German actor Curt Jurgens, who experienced clinical death during a complicated operation by Dr. Michael DeBakey, had a negative encounter:

"The feeling of well-being that I had shortly after the pentothal injection did not last long. Soon a feeling that life was ebbing from me rose up from my subconscious. Feeling my life draining away evoked powerful sensations of dread. I wanted to hold on to life more than anything.

"I had been looking up into the big glass cupola over the operating room. This cupola now began to change. Suddenly it turned a glowing red. I saw twisted faces grimacing as they stared down at me. . . . I tried to struggle upright and defend myself. . . . Then it seemed as if the glass cupola had turned into a transparent dome that was slowly sinking down over me. A fiery rain was now falling, but though the drops were enormous, none of them touched me. They splattered down around me, and out of them grew menacing tongues of flames. . . . I could no longer shut out the frightful truth: beyond doubt, the faces dominating this fiery world were the faces of the damned. I had a feeling of despair, of being unspeakably alone and abandoned. The sensation of horror was so great that it choked me, and I had the impression that I was about to suffocate. Obviously, I was in Hell itself."

Curt Jurgens saw no brilliant lights or friendly spirits, nor did he experience the peace and tranquility characteristic of most death encounters. Out of more than one thousand deathbed observations in the United States and in India, Dr. Osis found only one case where a patient saw "hell." The woman was an Italian-born housewife from Rhode Island. Her vision occurred after a gall-bladder operation. Her physician recalled:

"When she came to, she said, 'I thought I was dead, I was in hell.' Her eyes were popping out with fear. 'My God, I thought I was in hell.' After I reassured her, she told me about her experience in hell and said that the devil would take her. This was interspersed with descriptions of her sins and what people thought about her. As her fear increased, the nurses had difficulty holding her down. She became almost psychotic and her mother had to be called in to quiet her. She had long-standing guilt feelings, possibly stemming from . . . an extramarital relationship which resulted in illegitimate children. Her sister's death from the same illness scared her. She believed that God was punishing her for her sins."

Admittedly, such cases are rare. But if even one person has a hellish death encounter, it leaves open the hypothesis that, as all religions teach, death is not bliss for everyone. In fact, it seems irresponsible to assume that the manner in which a person lives his life does not in some way influence his death imagery and the hereafter he perceives. As psychologist Charles Garfield, who counsels dying patients, said, "There are as many different death-styles as there are life-styles."

It is clear that there has not been enough research on the negative hallucinations of the dying. The problem is compounded by the fact that so few negative hallucinations are reported. Where evidence is available we will examine negative death encounters, but the remainder of Part I will concern positive death encounters—those of the Second, Third, and Fourth Kinds.

2

Death Encounters of the Second Kind

We have defined this category to include people who have been clinically dead, medically unconscious, or in a severe life-threatening situation, and can later produce evidence to support the parasensory nature of their experience. At the very least, such evidence is proof of the telepathic, clairvoyant, and precognitive abilities of the human mind. At its best, such evidence strongly suggests that every human has an astral, or etheric double, and that in life-threatening situations, and at the moment of death, the astral body separates from the physical. Proof of the astral body's existence, and its behavior at the time of death, is the first step toward proving that we survive bodily death. In taking that step, we will examine three cases of Death Encounters of the Second Kind.

Barbara Pryor, age thirty-nine, is the wife of former Arkansas governor David Pryor. On Thanksgiving Day 1971, Barbara Pryor suffered a pulmonary embolism —a blood clot in her lung—following an emergency hysterectomy in a Washington, D.C., hospital. Her doctor, Donald Payne, said of Barbara's condition: "It was a very dangerous situation. We had to institute heroic measures to revive Mrs. Pryor." Here is what Barbara experienced:

"My spirit started rising in the air. I was at peace. The feeling was magnificent. I saw my body on the bed, but I felt completely detached from it. I really didn't care what they did to my body.

"I saw Dr. Payne beating on my chest, and I kept wondering, Why are you working so hard? I am completely and utterly happy. A man I had never seen before came to my body and administered a shot to the heart. When he finished, a nurse rushed up to the bed and in her haste knocked over the pole holding the bottles of intravenous fluid. I watched the pole fall onto the bed and saw one of the bottles hit the side of my face. But I didn't care about the bottle hitting me. I was free of all pain.

"Then I had the strangest feeling that at any second I would find my brother, who had died of leukemia the year before, right next to me."

Barbara sensed her brother's presence, and was about to turn around to see him when she suddenly heard Dr. Payne shouting, "Breathe, Barbara! Breathe!"

" 'Oh no I won't. You can't make me breathe. You can't make me leave this paradise.' Just as I said that, a searing pain rushed through my chest and instinctively I knew I had returned to my body. I felt trapped and angry for being forced to return. If there had been any way to stop the doctors, I would have done it."

An analysis of Barbara Pryor's case yields three pieces of evidence of Death Encounters of the Second

Kind: (1) Dr. Payne did administer manual cardiac massage in the manner in which Barbara "saw" it; (2) a second doctor did suddenly burst into the room and give Barbara an injection into her heart; (3) a nurse quickly approached Barbara's bed, and her elbow hit the pole and accidentally knocked over the intravenous bottles, which struck the left side of Barbara's face. When Barbara regained consciousness she had a painful bruise by her left eye—exactly where she had "seen" the bottle hit her. Barbara was definitely unconscious during all these activities; in fact, she was clinically dead. Yet, she accurately perceived the events around her—events that have been verified by hospital staff members.

Barbara Pryor saw events in the vicinity of her bed, but distance is apparently no obstacle for a clinically dead patient. Barbara Morris Davidson, age thirty-six, accidentally took an overdose of sleeping pills on the evening of April 21, 1975. She was rushed to Shallowbard Community Hospital in Atlanta, Georgia, where she was admitted unconscious and close to death. Dr. Walter Head, her attending physician, reported that Barbara remained comatose for three days. It was during this period of unconsciousness that she left her body and acquired information of the Second Kind.

Barbara recalled that at one point she saw doctors and nurses leaning over a body that she could not identify. Curious, she bent over the body and checked the name on the wristband. The patient was herself. Next, Barbara found herself viewing her body from across the room. Ironically, her location did not disturb her but her womanly pride bristled at the fact that the wristband gave her birthdate as December 23, 1940—making her two years older than she actually was. Piqued, Barbara tried to tell the nurses about the error, shouting at them, but they could not hear her. Finally she decided to go home and tell her husband about the frustrating mix-up. She was born on December 23, 1942—didn't the hospital realize that! Barbara recalled:

"I walked all the way home, astonished that my bare feet never touched the pavement. I realized then that I wasn't actually walking but floating.

"When I arrived home, I found my husband sleeping in a living-room chair, with a picture of me lying nearby. I tried to wake him, but he wouldn't stir, so I decided to return to the hospital.

The next thing Barbara remembered was opening her eyes and seeing doctors and nurses staring down at her. Only later did she learn that she had been in a coma for three days—and that her heart had stopped beating for a while.

While recuperating, Barbara told her husband about her strange journey home. He confirmed that one evening while she lay comatose in the hospital, he was so worried about her and so lonely that he took a framed picture of her and sat in their living room staring at it. He remembered awakening to find the picture clutched in his arms. This fact made Barbara curious about her experience, which until then she had thought was pure fantasy. As soon as she was well, she returned to the hospital and requested permission to examine her hospital records. At the top of the first page she found her birthdate incorrectly given as December 23, 1940.

It is interesting to note that neither Barbara Pryor nor Barbara Davidson saw bright light, heard voices or music, or met spirits. Nor have many others who had Death Encounters of the Second Kind. At this early stage of thanatological research, we can only speculate why this is so. It may be that the visual and auditory stimuli that characterize a Death Encounter of the First Kind are so spectacular and hypnotic that they almost entirely consume the individual's awareness. So mesmerized by the otherworldly aspects of his experience, the person seems totally disinterested in worldly scenes or in attempting to contact friends or family. Perhaps the person who has a Death Encounter of the First Kind is farther along the route to permanent, irreversible death—perhaps he is "more dead" than the person who can still be concerned with earthly business. It seems a logical assumption, and one that could be verified if researchers attempted to correlate the kind of Death Encounter a person has with the medical facts that would determine his "degree" of death—that is, a measure of the seriousness of his condition and the probability that he could be revived.

Experiences like Barbara Pryor's and Barbara Davidson's occur not only during clinical death. That fact offers scientists one way to study—and even to stage—death encounters. Richard Heath, age forty-seven, of Olympia, Washington, underwent surgery on his right knee on May 17, 1971. While still drugged from his operation at Tacoma Washington Central Hospital, he had an OBE that generated factual parasensory information. Richard recalled:

"Suddenly my body became extremely relaxed. I felt my spirit separate from my earthly body and rise toward the ceiling. Then I found myself floating through the sky toward my home. It was a beautiful day and the trip was very pleasant.

"When I arrived home, I saw the children playing in our yard. My attention was drawn to a neighbor's yard. I saw—casually, without realizing how important it would be to me later—that he was planting two small trees.

"Then I began to worry about my body, back at the hospital. How would I get back? But no sooner had the notion entered my mind than I

35

was back, with a painful flash, inside my injured body. I opened my eyes, feeling extremely exhausted and thinking what a weird dream I had had."

The first day home, on crutches, Richard hobbled over to his neighbor's. He was flabbergasted to see two new saplings exactly where he had "seen" them being planted. He told his neighbor about the experience and the neighbor gave Richard one of the trees. The tree is almost eight years old now, and Richard Heath frequently sits outside on his porch, listening to the wind blow through the branches, assured in his belief that the spirit can travel outside the body and that the spirit therefore survives bodily death.

There is strong evidence that OBEs and some aspects of clinical death are in many ways related. OBEs are conducive to a whole range of ESP phenomena, and many people who experience clinical death later report having a residual telepathic or clairvoyant sense. Sandra Carey, a writer, entered a West Coast hospital in the winter of 1970 with a terminal disease and shortly thereafter her heart stopped beating. She was clinically dead for four minutes. When she regained consciousness, she told her attending doctor that she felt fine but was sad for him because his wife had recently left him and was going to file for divorce. The doctor was astonished. His wife had indeed left him, but just two days before, and he had taken extreme care that no one at the hospital know this. In fact, not even his family knew about the breakup yet. Sandra, who is healthy today, claims that on certain occasions she still possesses a telepathic sense that is a result of her encounter with death. She accounts for it this way: "Once you break through the normal dimensions of space and time, you realize they *can* be broken and this knowledge leaves you open to paranormal phenomena." Unfortunately, no researcher has yet attempted to determine the number of people who have been resuscitated from clinical death and subsequently experience paranormal perceptions. It would make an interesting and enlightening study.

Many researchers have considered the question of how people like Barbara Pryor, Barbara Davidson, and Richard Heath acquired their paranormal information. Barbara Davidson and Richard Heath both felt that they actually traveled several miles. The sensation of astral travel is very real to anyone who has experienced it; these people are convinced that the essence of their personality journeys *in toto* from the site of their body to a remote location. But some psychical researchers wonder if this indeed happens. Might human consciousness, under certain extreme circumstances, simply transcend space and time and perceive events clairvoyantly? In other words, is there difference between astral travel and clairvoyant perception?

This question is of vital import to researchers who are interested in the issue of survival. Clairvoyant perception might be a talent inherent in a person's mind and vanish when that person dies. Proof of astral travel, however, would mean that every material body has an etheric double that is the essense of life itself and can live after the physical body has died.

In order to answer our question, researchers are studying OBEs in a variety of new ways. The eminent British researcher Dr. Robert Crookall has diligently collected reports of over a thousand OBEs and analyzed his data for common denominators that would reveal something about the nature of OBEs. Crookall has found that out-of-body accounts display six characteristics:

1. The person feels he is leaving his body through the top of his head.
2. At the instant of separation of the etheric and

physical bodies, the person momentarily blacks out.

3. Before wandering, the etheric body hovers for some time over the physical shell.
4. When the etheric body returns from its travels, it goes through the hovering position again.
5. A blackout occurs at the moment of reintegration.
6. Rapid reentry jolts the physical body and can elevate heartrate and induce profuse sweating.

Crookall has found no cases of people being unable to reunite their physical and etheric bodies (or if there were, no one lived to report it). Regardless of how far the etheric body travels, the person's fear acts as a hook to yank the spirit back and merge it with the physical.

In one well-known long-distance experiment, the famous psychic Mrs. Eileen Garrett projected herself from New York to a town in Iceland at a predetermined time and observed the actions of experimenter Dr. D. Svenson. In a semitrance state she reported exactly what Svenson was doing. She saw him reading a book, and she described the text, a bandage he had wrapped around his head, and the room. When asked how she had perceived the information, Mrs. Garrett tried to extricate herself from the logistical dilemma by saying that she did not practice either astral travel or clairvoyant perception, but "traveling clairvoyance."

Psychics maintain that the astral and physical bodies are connected by a slender, glistening silver cord, an infinitely elastic tether running from the top of the head of the physical body to the same location on the etheric double. As long as the silver cord remains intact, so the story goes, the astral body can always return to the physical. No experiment has yet detected a silver thread, but its existence could offer an explanation of why some resuscitation efforts fail and others succeed. If a clinically dead person decides to continue his journey toward the light, the moment he decides not to return to his body, the silver cord would be severed. In psychic parlance, a severed silver cord is synonymous with permanent death.

Psychologist Dr. Charles Tart of the University of California, Davis, has studied OBEs and pondered the question of whether we all have astral doubles that can travel and obtain information. In August 1966, Dr. Tart had eight laboratory sessions with Virginia businessman Robert Monroe, who is adept at inducing OBEs. Dr. Tart electronically monitored Monroe's brainwaves, eye movements, and heartrate while Monroe tried to travel out of his body to read a five-digit number that was on a shelf in an adjacent room. Unfortunately, conditions were far from ideal. An army cot served as the bed, and a clip-type ear electrode clung to Monroe's earlobe like a baby alligator. On the final night of the experiment Monroe had two OBEs. In one trip he saw several people he did not recognize standing in an unfamiliar location: nothing verifiable. In the second one he had great difficulty controlling himself; he could not enter the adjacent room to read the target number. His etheric body, he said, seemed to drift of its own free will out of the laboratory and into a hallway of the building. On awakening three minutes later, Monroe said that he had seen a woman laboratory technician talking with a man. Dr. Tart checked the hall and found this to be true.

Two years later Dr. Tart had more success working with Monroe. Although he still could not read the target number, he often provided bits of information of events taking place in other parts of the buildings—all of which turned out to be correct. Most importantly, during the periods that Monroe was wandering out of his body, Dr. Tart observed definite physiological changes. Monroe's blood pressure dropped, his eye movements increased, and his brainwave pattern switched to prolonged theta rhythms, waves typical of yogis in deep meditation. However, Dr. Tart could not draw any conclusions as to how Monroe obtained his paranormal information. Nor could Dr. Karlis Osis, as late as 1973, draw definite conclusions in his experiments with psychic Ingo Swann at the American Society for Psychical Research in New York City. Swann was put through a battery of tests and his brainwaves were monitored while he tried to discern target objects in an open box that hung from the ceiling above his head. Swann had a phenomenal success, scoring eight direct hits out of eight different targets—with odds of one in forty thousand. Dr. Osis observed a twenty-percent loss in Swann's brainwave activity during the experiments, but he could not conclude whether some part of Swann's spirit actually rose and peered over the rim of the box—which Swann claimed was the way in which he saw the targets.

Not until the mid-1970s did any researcher succeed in determining whether we all have astral bodies. The first experiment was conducted by physicists at the Energy Research Group in New York City, using the talents of psychic Dr. Alex Tanous. It proved to be more than the scientists had bargained for, and it has provided some of the best laboratory evidence for survival of the spirit after death. Dr. Tanous and the experiment are worth considering in detail.

Alex Tanous, a psychic with a Ph.D. in theology, can have OBEs at will. He has counseled dying patients and has seen mists and vapors form around a person before death—vapors that ascend from the body at the moment of death. After Tanous witnessed his brother David's OBE at the time of his death in 1957, he joined the staff of Holy Ghost Hospital in Boston. The hospital is for patients with incurable diseases, and there Tanous used his psychic sensitivity to study death first-hand. "On many occasions," he said, "I saw a shapeless mist drift away from a patient when he died."

In 1972 Tanous was contacted by Dr. Osis with a special request: Osis's organization, the American Society for Psychical Research, had, on December 29, 1972, been awarded $270,000 to find proof of the human soul. The money had been left in 1946 by an Arizona gold prospector who had stipulated, in his will, that his estate be spent for "research for some scientific proof of a soul of the human body which leaves at death." His will was discovered in 1964, and after lengthy legal battles the Arizona Supreme Court awarded money to the ASPR.

In court, the ASPR had put forth the hypothesis that "some part of the human personality indeed is capable of operating outside the living body [becoming ecsomatic] on rare occasions, and that it may continue to exist after the brain processes have ceased and the organism is decayed." The organization said it would test this hypothesis in several ways, one of which was to study the ecsomatic experiences—OBEs—of living people. After winning the so-called Kidd Legacy, the ASPR staff tested many people who claimed they could have OBEs, and Alex Tanous proved, quite literally, to be their glowing star.

The "fly-in" experiments, as they were called, required Tanous to astrally project himself from his home in Portland, Maine, to a room in the ASPR building on Manhattan's West Side. He was to scan a coffee table on which were several objects, then call the ASPR with his report. Here is Tanous's account of his first series of fly-ins:

"I underwent five separate trials. One time, I had the definite impression that something was wrong with the table. I saw an odd separation between various objects and colors. When Vera Feldman, an ASPR researcher, called me, I told her what I'd seen.

41

" 'That's amazing,' she said. 'The table was divided into two parts. We kept some objects on one side purposely. But what objects did you see?'

"I saw a candle. And something wrapped around it, like a ribbon. Also, there was a piece of wood."

" 'My God!' Vera said. 'You're right.'

"On another occasion, I flew in and saw a basket of fruit. I was right again. On a later flight, I saw a knife lying on the table. It turned out to be a letter opener. On yet another occasion, I saw Vera drinking a cup of tea. She later confirmed that she'd been drinking tea in Dr. Osis's office at the time. And on my fifth trial, I once again saw Vera. This time, she bent over the table I was looking at. Again, she confirmed this by phone."

On each occasion Tanous viewed the table by hovering above it—the same way clinically dead patients report seeing their own resuscitation. Encouraged by Tanous's success, one evening the ASPR staff got reknown psychic Christine Whiting to sit in the room and see if she could sense when Tanous was present. He was not told that she would be there. Whiting did more than sense Tanous's presence: she actually saw him, first as a ball of light, then later, she accurately described what he was wearing at the time he astrally projected himself from his home in Maine.

The ball of light intrigued the ASPR staff. Light supposedly composed the halos of saints. Light is also supposed to be the essence of spirit entities. People occasionally "light up"—literally and figuratively—at the moment of death. Light plays a major role in the stories of patients revived from clinical death. In fact, Tanous had repeatedly said that during his OBEs: "I consist of a large spot of light, a glowing ball of consciousness, which gradually gets smaller and more concentrated. This is how I travel. As light."

Light is an easily detectable form of energy. Some physicists began to wonder if equipment could record Tanous's astral body as light. If so, this would be the most conclusive proof to date of an entity—or energy form—that can separate itself from the physical body and possibly survive it. A fulfillment of the Kidd Legacy. A major scientific discovery.

Arrangements were made to use the facilities of the Energy Research Group, a branch of the Institute for Bioenergetic Analysis, located on Grand Street in New York City. The organization is composed of biochemists, physicists, medical doctors, and psychiatrists attempting to study the electromagnetic nature of psychic phenomena. For their experiment with Tanous, the ERG used a specially designed room that was theoretically black. It contained a photomultiplier tube, a highly sensitive device that can detect a few photons of light. Target objects were placed on a chair in the center of the room. Tanous not only had to trigger the photomultiplier tube with a burst of his inner light, but also he had to identify the targets. He asked for a small, dark room in which he could concentrate and from which he could project himself into the experimental chamber; comically, the only room available was the men's bathroom. Once sequestered there, Tanous's voice was tape-recorded:

"I am sitting in the john . . . and I'm to astral project into a very dark room which I have seen. I will now breathe quite heavily. . . . I'm going to slump into the chair, kind of put my feet against the wall. . . . [Later] A ball of light is beginning to appear in my mind. I'm projecting myself now. . . . I'm trying to come down to hit the target on the chair. One of the targets is on the floor and it's square to me. I'm touching something. It's as if it were soft, like leather. The object on the chair is hard. It's circular, clear or white. . . .

43

"My light is getting smaller. The target on the floor seems to be closer to the wall, the left side. . . . Pow! There's a burst of light. The object on the floor feels like it's a wallet. The one on the chair is tall, circular—by circular, meaning it appears circular, as if it were a statue. . . . [Long silence] Pow! An explosion of white! I'm dangling, dangling, dangling. . . ."

New York psychiatrist Carl Kirsh and researcher Ted Wolfe of the New York Medical Center finally got Tanous from the men's room (the experiment had taken twenty-one minutes) and brought him into the black chamber, which now was normally lighted. On the chair was a tall, circular heating element from a coffeepot, just as Tanous had described it. On the floor lay a smooth rubber pad, exactly where Tanous had said he thought a wallet was located. Most impressively, the photomultiplier tube had registered light in the room, energy that flared during the exact times Tanous shouted, "Pow! There's a burst of light."

If every person possesses a detachable light component, then the existence of astral bodies would be a universal reality. Since the work with Tanous, other psychics as well as ordinary people have bodily entered the chamber and stood naked in front of the phototube. Astonishingly, to some degree, everyone glows! The naked body does have a visible brilliance. It is too weak for ordinary eyes to see, but it can be glimpsed by the sensitive eyes of psychics, and now it has been detected by scientific equipment. What's more, the all-encompassing halo is magnificently colored (as psychics have always insisted), pulsates at definite frequencies, and assumes different geometric configurations that seem to correspond to a person's psychological and physical conditions.

One New York City doctor, adept at yogic breathing exercises, was able to increase his "shine" more than five hundred percent. He believes that this offers proof to the claim of mystics that psychic energy, which they call *prana,* can be tapped by anyone through meditation and breathing. Some people glow more than others. The reasons for this are not yet understood. Does a strong glow mean that a person is more spiritually oriented than someone with a faint shine? Does it mean that he or she will live longer? Does a weak glow indicate that death is near? At this time we know only that the glow appears to stem from the astral body, and that people who can have OBEs can project their "ball of light" over great distances in a flash, and return as quickly— as long as the silver thread remains intact. The existence of the silver thread has not yet been proved, but something must connect the physical and astral bodies. Could the brilliant light reported by the clinically dead be the collective shine of thousands upon thousands of spirits? It is too early to try to answer that question. But we do know that light has always played a major role in religion and myth, and now, for the first time, it seems that we are beginning to understand why.

3
Death Encounters of the Third Kind

We have defined this category to include clinically dead or unconscious people who convey to other persons a "gut feeling" concerning their condition. There is contact—perhaps by some form of ESP—between a "dead" or dying person and a living human being. The person whose life hangs in the balance does not have to travel astrally to deliver his message; the danger is conveyed telepathically.

The most distinguishing characteristic of this kind of encounter is that the recipient of the message generally has only a vague idea that something is wrong with someone with whom he or she is acquainted. They usually do not know with any certainty who the person is or what the life-threatening situation is about. Most importantly, they never feel that they are in paranormal communication with anyone. From research in parapsychology it seems that the death message is received at a subliminal level of the mind, and that for various reasons, only fragments of it surface to conscious awareness. In some cases it is clear that the death message would be too painful in its suddenness, and a "mental filter" protects the recipient by gradually leaking out the information. Never does the recipient suspect that he or she is in contact with a dying or clinically dead individual (that would constitute a Death Encounter of the Fourth Kind). The case of Martha Egan and her mother is one example of a Death Encounter of the Third Kind. The case of Wallace Abel, formerly a professor of communications at the University of Arizona and now a journalist, is an even more vivid example of this phenomenon.

Wallace Abel's story is well documented. It has been confirmed by family members, doctors, and nurses who attended Abel during his sickness, and has been recorded in the files of the Scottsdale Memorial Hospital in Arizona.

Shortly before 6:00 A.M., August 30, 1975, less than two weeks after his forty-ninth birthday, Wallace Abel collapsed at his home. His breathing and pulse stopped and he was rushed to the emergency room of Scottsdale Memorial Hospital. Cardiologist Dr. Marvin Goldstein used a defibrillator to shock Abel back to life. Abel had been dead, but he recalls nothing of his first brush with death.

Then, early on Tuesday, September 2, while still in the hospital, Abel's heart went into spasm. Nurses administered drugs, but after a while Abel stopped responding. According to one nurse: "He began to hallucinate. I had the impression that he was bargaining with the Lord for his life, that he wasn't ready to go yet." The doctors agreed that Abel was dying, and chaplain Dr. L. Wilson Kilgore of the Valley Presbyterian Church was called by Abel's wife, Lee. Wallace Abel still vividly remembers this confrontation with death:

"Suddenly there was a tugging at my midsection. A transparent figure of me was struggling to leave my body. I recognized it immediately. But

47

my body seemed to refuse to let go of this cloud of me. My image struggled, twisted, pulled. Suddenly I realized I was witnessing my own struggle for life."

Several hundred miles away, at the campus of Texas Technical University, Abel's twenty-year-old daughter, Clare, was on her way to her 11:00 A.M. class. Suddenly a strange feeling washed over her. Clare told us:

"I got the sensation that I didn't have time to attend that class. Or any other that day. It was ridiculous, because this particular day I had no other plans. The feeling was so strong, and so strange, that I just sort of drifted back to my dorm. I'd say my mind was a blank.

"Entering the building, I first got a sickening feeling that something was wrong, but I didn't know what. Then I saw a group of kids at the far end of the hall near my room. I felt a pain in my chest, a sharp pain, and my breath was cut short. I raced down the hall and saw that the door to my room was plastered with notes for me to call home. An emergency."

Clare knew of her father's previous heart attack, and although the notes on her door contained no specifics, she concluded that the emergency concerned her father. "I thought he had died," she said.

Clare called home and was told by neighbors that her father was only sick, that it was nothing serious but she should come home immediately. This confirmed her worst suspicion. "Now I was sure he was dead," she recalled. Unable to get a plane to Arizona until 5:00 P.M., she sat in her room and cried. Meanwhile, at the hospital, Wallace Abel had two distinct visions:

"A scene appeared like a slide. I found myself floating on my back on a still lake. The soles of my feet did not quite reach the shore, where my family stood. They were looking at me distressfully. I raised my hand to reach out for them. They responded, but our hands couldn't touch. It seemed hopeless, and I let my hand fall to my side. I wanted particularly to touch my daughter Clare, the one I've always felt the closest to.

"The scene changed to a valley, then again to another valley. What I was seeing close at hand was far more stimulating than the previous scene. Inside I could feel a compulsion stirring, urging me to get closer and see more. One foot already was through a gate. The urge to bring the other forward swelled to the point where I felt I no longer could resist it. Just as I was about to take that second step, some inner awareness flashed a message. I knew that if I took that step it would not be a matter merely of satisfying curiosity or some strange sensation. Somehow I understood that there would be no coming back.

"The comprehension began sweeping over me that I was experiencing something rare, something that few people had been privileged to view. I had seen beyond life, and the consciousness hit me full force."

At that moment Abel opened his eyes and shouted, "Where's Clare? I can't go without Clare!" His eyes swept the room. Standing at the foot of his bed were his wife, Lee, his youngest daughter, Stacey, fifteen, and his eldest daughter, Vicki, twenty-three. Clare was missing. "Clare is my carbon copy," Abel told us in the spring of 1977, "in looks, in temperament, and in mannerisms. She is so close to me that in childhood she would make remarks or observations that were direct quotes of my own thoughts at the same age. Many I'd even forgotten until she dredged them up."

Clare too has always felt unusually close to her

49

father. In college she had tried to take a major other than her father's specialty, mass communications, but eventually she shifted to that field. "We're exactly alike in every respect," she remarked.

Clare's plane from El Paso arrived an hour late at Sky Harbor Airport. Friends sped her to the hospital. On seeing her, her father said calmly, "Hi, honey, it's good to see you." Then he drifted into a state of semiconsciousness. "Peace swept over me," Abel remembers. After twenty-four hours he was out of crisis. Today, Wallace Abel is certain that he somehow contacted his daughter while he was unconscious. In retrospect, Clare is equally sure that her strange behavior that morning in September was prompted by a psychic alert from her father.

Physical communication between family members, or lovers, is not uncommon. The natural intimacy of a relationship seems to serve as a bridge for telepathic contact. The contact is strongest at the two ends of life's spectrum—birth and death. In an outstanding experiment conducted in a Moscow obstetrics clinic, mothers were kept in a remote wing of a building. It was impossible for a mother to hear the cries of her baby, and there was no way for her to know when a doctor was attending the infant. Yet, when a baby cried as a doctor took a blood specimen, its mother showed measurable signs of anxiety. The Soviet study documented numerous clear-cut cases of mother-infant telepathy. One of the most dramatic cases of mother-child communication we found turned out also to be a Death Encounter of the Third Kind.

In March 1959, Michele Hauser, a fifty-five-year-old housewife now living in Florida, was severely ill with the flu. She had a high fever for three days and was confined to bed. For convenience, she placed a bed in the living room of her New York City home. Her daughter, Connie, then age twelve, was in bed upstairs when suddenly she got a strong feeling that her mother was going to die. As an excuse to talk with her, Connie called downstairs for a glass of water. Her mother brought the water upstairs, and Connie recalled: "I knew that when she got back downstairs she would die. Yet I was too frightened to say anything to her."

Mrs. Hauser returned to the living room and climbed into her daybed. Her husband was working the night shift that week. With no warning, she suddenly sensed that she was going to die. Then she was out of her body.

"I was able to see myself. I all at once felt myself soaring up into space. Faster and faster I went. Space was like a dark void, but it wasn't black. It was like nothing at all. I've never been able to find the right words to describe the void I flew through.

"The void around death is strange. I didn't feel the passage of time. I only felt that I was moving toward something. What it was I don't know. There was no sound at all. It was a strange experience, but even stranger, I liked it. It was definitely pleasant. I certainly wasn't afraid.

"I glimpsed myself on the bed, and I still remember the brilliant white sheets. Suddenly I thought about my three children."

Her greatest concern was that she was going to leave her children. She had two boys younger than Connie. She shouted, "Please, God, my husband is Protestant and I'm Catholic. Let me live so that I can raise my children as Catholics." Three times Michele pleaded, and on the third supplication she heard a response: "You can stay awhile longer. It is 4:25, and someone else must go in your place." She felt relieved. "Then a sudden and tremendous smack like a giant slap struck me—my doctor says it was my soul returning to my body." When she awakened, she glanced at the bedside clock: it read 4:25 A.M. She then said a prayer for the person who had died in her place.

While Michele Hauser was having this experience, upstairs, young Connie was having one of her own:

"I saw in my mind that my mother was dying. I saw her rising above her body on the bed. I was terrified, and knew that there was nothing I could do to help. Her spirit floated in the living room. I tried to shake the image from my head, but nothing would erase it. Her spirit disappeared, and for two hours I just lay in bed, afraid that if I went downstairs I would find my mother's corpse."

Ten years passed before Connie or her mother mentioned what they had lived through that night. When they did talk about it, they were amazed at the many similarities between their stories. Mrs. Hauser told us: "It was as though Connie had actually lived the experience I was having. She described everything I went through, and almost everything I felt. This was the first and only psychic thing that ever happened between us."

The ties between a mother and her child are particularly strong. We know that the physical ties are total; in the intimacy of the womb, the floating fetus is one with the mother. There is no aspect of the new life that is independent. The mother's body chemistry, diet, habits of drinking, smoking, pill-taking, and exercising —all mold the intrauterine child. Even the mother's temperament throughout pregnancy is subtly reflected in the baby's makeup. Beyond these obvious physical ties, say parapsychologists, are incontestable psychical ties. Philosopher Henri Bergson called it the "special sympathy between mother and child." Doctors have routinely observed this special sympathy, scientists are currently trying to measure it, and all mothers have experienced it.

Scientists believe that the ability to communicate telepathically is innate. But usually this subtle, delicate mode of communication is swamped by the everyday inputs to our senses. "We probably receive many telepathic messages from friends and relatives every day," said Charles Honorton, director of the Maimonides Medical Center in Brooklyn, a leading institute for psychical research. "Because the messages probably do not have a strong emotional impact, they never rise to the surface of awareness. It usually takes a traumatic event to break through." If that is true, it is no wonder that messages concerning death hit their mark. Aside from birth, death is the most traumatic event in life. Michele Hauser and her daughter Connie broke the psychical-communication barrier only when one of them was literally on her deathbed. Only then did the message rise above the noise of ordinary sensory stimuli.

Dr. Berthold Schwarz, a New Jersey psychiatrist and a former Fellow in Psychiatry at the May Foundation, has a deep interest in the special psychical communications between parent and child. Over the last ten years he has documented more than fifteen hundred cases of this intimate form of communication. Not all his cases contain death messages—in fact, few do; what Dr. Schwartz has done is try to filter out the subtler messages that are present but often go unnoticed. His premise is that if we can become aware of the simpler messages, then the truly important ones may have a better chance of registering with us.

According to Dr. Schwarz, most instances of parent–child telepathy go unnoticed because they occur in the context of everyday experiences. Schwarz and his wife, Ardis, did not want to overlook any possible telepathic interchanges in their own household; therefore, they decided to undertake a careful study of the actions of their two children, Eric and Lisa. "With the passing of time," says Dr. Schwarz, "my wife and I became skilled in recognizing what really went on in the family in a nonverbal, subliminal, telepathic way." What really went on became the nucleus of Dr. Schwarz's book, *Parent-Child Telepathy*. Here is an incident that occurred a week before Christmas:

> "My intention of writing 'first-class mail' on an important letter that had to go out right away was completely frustrated because there was no red pen on my desk. My search for it was to no avail. My thoughts went: 'Oh, I suppose Ardis took it for the Christmas cards and never returned it.' At that moment Eric (age three) bounded downstairs and into my office. 'Here, Daddy, is the red pen!' "

As an isolated incident, of course, this experience means nothing. Coincidence, we say. And that is just the point Dr. Schwarz strives to emphasize. The incident, he said, could easily have been overlooked or interpreted as mere coincidence, but that would have masked its significance. For as Dr. Schwarz and his wife began to faithfully record such seemingly trivial experiences, they found that Eric anticipated their wishes quite often. One day Ardis, who was upstairs in her bedroom, decided to hang a certain picture on the kitchen wall where a calendar was then hanging. She came downstairs with the picture, went into the kitchen, and found Eric up on a chair, removing the calendar from the wall. When she asked him why he had done it at precisely that moment, he could give no answer.

Dr. Schwarz points out that each incident in itself was so minor that without a written record, one event would have been forgotten before the next occurred. On paper, as accumulated events, they strongly suggested that Eric had a telepathic sense when it came to reading his parents' thoughts. If so many trivial messages reach us (albeit at a subliminal level), surely all the important ones arrives. Dr. Schwarz believes that if we make ourselves aware of the subtle telepathic messages, as he and his wife did, then when a serious one comes along we will have less trouble picking it out and deciphering it from the daily noise. To an open, perceptive mind, certainly a message of death should register clearly. That it does so infrequently may be a measure of our insensitivity—or our unwillingness to experience anything unpleasant.

We have found that people who have had encounters with death have very definite views on the subject. For one, Wallace Abel thinks that OBEs in the distant past were what initially gave our ancestors their first notion of spirits and of heaven. "Once you've been out of your body and experienced death," he said, "it is impossible not to be spiritually inclined." Abel feels that Jesus Christ's resurrection may have been similar to a present-day Death Encounter (one of the Fourth Kind, since Jesus was seen by his apostles). A person's consciousness, said Abel, lingers long after the body's vital life signs have disappeared; thus, doctors should wait at least forty-eight hours before pronouncing a person dead and putting his body in a freezer. "We might be knocking off thousands of people every year who are not fully or finally dead," said Abel. "People who could be brought back with just a little more effort on the part of doctors, people who are conscious of the fact that their body has been pronounced dead and that their doctors have given up on them." This is a real and frightening prospect, and we will give it considerable attention in Part II.

The case of Wallace Abel is a perfect example of a Death Encounter of the Third Kind. Initially, his daughter Clare had only a vague feeling that something terrible had happened. For talented psychic Ingo Swann, the death message was equally as unclear. In 1964 Swann was walking down Sullivan Street in New York City's Greenwich Village. It was a clear, sunny day. Suddenly Swann felt faint and experienced a pain in the left side of his head. He fell over and tore his pants on the pavement, cutting his left knee. "I was not unconscious," he said, "but in a groggy, semiaware state. When I regained my composure, I had the distinct feeling that someone close to me had just died. But I couldn't think who. Since my grandmother was the oldest member of the family, I sort of naturally concluded that it was she."

A few hours later Swann received a call from the West Coast. His father had died of a stroke. Swann had correctly perceived a death, but even his psychic sensitivity had not zeroed in on the person who had died. There is another dimension to Swann's story. The stroke had occurred on the left side of his father's brain—the same side where Swann had felt the sharp pain. In a later conversation with a member of his family, Swann learned that his father had fallen to the ground and badly cut his left knee—the same knee Swann had cut in his fall.

Ingo Swann is not mystified by his experience. He feels that it was quite natural for his father's death to be broadcast to him. If anything, he finds it embarrassing that he did not decipher the psychic message more clearly. Since then, Swann has had his own personal rendezvous with death, and he found it to be strikingly similar to the many OBEs he has produced, at will, for scientists to study. Swann's Death Encounter occurred in 1972 in Palo Alto, California. Swann was suffering from a mild infection for which a local doctor administered a shot of penicillin. He had never before been allergic to the drug, but this time he went into shock. He was rushed to the Palo Alto Medical Center and pronounced dead on arrival. For about twenty minutes doctors worked to revive him. Since he had often traveled out of his body, he was not at all frightened by the fact that he was viewing his corpse from a distance. He did not know whether the doctors could successfully resuscitate him, but this too did not disturb him.

He did not fear death. Instead, analytical-minded as he is, Swann decided to take advantage of this unique opportunity to compare clinical death with his past OBEs. Today he recalls that "the common features are truly amazing," but cautions that "this is not to say that the two experiences are identical." Visual perception was the same for Swann. He found that he could change his point of perspective at will, viewing things from the ceiling, for instance, just as he does in an OBE; and mobility was also the same. "You have only to will yourself to a particular location in space, and you're there," he said. But Swann believes that the emotions people experience during clinical death depend largely on their attitude toward life. "I experienced no fear during any stage of my death," he said, "but then I had been out of my body hundreds of times since childhood."

Swann believes strongly that OBEs are rehearsals for ultimate death, and that the more mini-deaths a person can experience, the easier will be final death. We will see that that belief is supported by several recent scientific studies.

4

Premonitions
of Death

Have you ever felt that someone was about to die, and they did? Have you ever dreamed of someone's death, only to find that that dream came true? If so, then you may have participated in a Death Encounter of the Third Kind. Their existence, and the evidence we have examined in the preceding chapter, poses an important question: Is the ability to predict death an innate, though largely latent, human talent?

In December 1970, Linda Wilson, a New Jersey housewife and mother, entered the home of a neighbor for a Christmas-season dinner and immediately felt uncomfortable. "I 'smelled' death," she reported. "Every time I inhaled, the inside of my nose seemed to freeze, as though I were outside in blistering weather." She found the smell "mildly sour," overpowering the fragrance of a pine Christmas tree and all the hot foods on the dining-room table. The husband of the woman hosting the dinner had Parkinson's disease, but no one, including his doctors, expected him to die. (In fact, the disease itself is not usually lethal.) Yet, Linda Wilson did not enjoy her dinner that night. "I stared at

Peter [the sick husband] all evening. It was crazy, but I knew he was going to die. He ate like an ox, and his complexion was ruddy, but every time I faced him I got a chill. Nothing like that ever happened to me before." One week later Pete came down with pneumonia. In five days he died of fluid in his lungs. Did Linda Wilson actually smell death? Does it have an odor?

We are told that death can be seen. One famous psychic told of seeing death while standing on an upper floor of a skyscraper, waiting for an elevator. When one arrived and the door opened, she stood back in terror. All four people in the elevator had no auras. A man boarded the elevator and immediately his glow vanished. "It's a sign of death," the psychic said. "I wanted to tell them all to get out, to take another car, but I knew nobody would listen." The door closed and the elevator plummeted twenty-two floors, killing the five people onboard. For some mysterious reason, the emergency brakes did not catch.

There is evidence that some animals can sense death. Rosalia Abreu, the first person ever to breed chimpanzees in captivity, told of an incident concerning the death of a female in her collection. At the moment that this chimp died in an indoor area, her mate, who was outside in the park, began to scream. "He continued to scream, looking about as though he saw something," and later, when another chimp died, he did the same thing. "He screamed and screamed and screamed. And he kept looking and looking, with lower lip hanging down, as if he saw something that we could not see. His scream was different from anything I have heard at other times. It made my flesh creep."

How do vultures locate a dying animal? We know that hyenas and jackals are attracted to the site of a dying animal by sounds and smells, "but vultures," reported biologist Lyall Watson, "seem to use some other cue and often zero in on even a hidden corpse with uncanny precision." Vultures do have superb eyesight, enhanced by a fine structure in front of the retina, which is designed to accentuate even the most distant movements. As soon as one vulture spots food, others come spiraling down in his wake. But sometimes this is not enough to explain their presence. Watson claimed: "I have seen vultures arriving in the dark to sit like impatient pallbearers around an antelope that had been shot, and on these occasions there were no mammalian scavengers around to attract their attention." He concludes, as many psychical researchers have, that a signal might go out from a dying organism and that this alarm is particularly strong when the attack on the organism is sudden and violent.

Clive Backster's work on what he calls "primary perception" in plants is well known, and it is worth looking at one of his most fascinating experiments. Backster is a polygraph (lie detector) expert and a highly controversial researcher. As one of the foremost authorities on the behavioral use of the lie detector, Backster was called before Congress in 1964 to testify on polygraph usage in government. At present, he is director of his own New York City school, which provides advanced training to law-enforcement officers in the techniques of the polygraph.

On the morning of February 2, 1966, Backster made an accidental discovery while doing some routine polygraph work at his school's offices near Times Square. He found that plants, when wired to a lie detector, seemed to sense when he approached them with the intent of doing them harm. The plants seemed to read his thoughts.

Months of testing began; all procedures were automated, and finally experiments were conducted. In one test, three philodendrons were placed in separate rooms. Each was wired to a polygraph and the room was sealed off. In another room, a large pot of boiling water was prepared. An instrument was programmed to dump a quantity of live brine shrimp into the water at a randomly selected time. No one was in the rooms with the plants, and no one knew exactly when the shrimp would be boiled alive. Backster's previous experiments had convinced him that plants were responsive to human thoughts; now he wondered if there was some fundamental communication between all living things. Would the plants respond to the mass death of the shrimp?

In this first test, two sessions totaling seven runs were conducted. Five to seven seconds after the shrimp were dumped into the boiling water, the polygraphs on all three plants showed sudden, large bursts of activity. Backster wondered: "Could it be that when cell life dies, it broadcasts a signal to other living cells?" Today, after seven years of experimentation, he feels sure of the answer. "I would say that whatever is abruptly killed must send out a message. A more orderly dying involves some preparation for death, and we've found that when this occurs there is little if any plant reaction." One wonders if this applies also to modes of human death, for sudden, violent, accidental deaths seem to be the ones most frequently detected by friends and family members.

Later, Backster found that his plants not only were attuned to dying shrimp but responded to all kinds of lifeforms. They reacted wildly to an egg being broken in the room. This suggested that plants are aware of all life forces, and that when those forces depart they send out signals in all directions—signals that can be picked up by perceptive receivers.

This is apparently what happened to two identical twins, Bobbie Jean and Betty Jo Eller, of Purlear, North Carolina. From the time of their birth the two girls were inseparable, so much so that they never truely became individuals. Betty Jo was the shadow of her sister in thoughts, desires, and actions. Whenever Bobbie Jean was sick, so too was her sister.

Shortly after the girls graduated from high school, their parents noticed that the personalities of Bobbie

Jean and Betty Jo had begun to change. Bobbie began sitting for hours staring into space, refusing to talk to anyone. And as always happened, her sister soon adopted the same bizarre pattern. As the girls, bound in their deep partnership, withdrew further from the outside world, they began to weep uncontrollably. They never left their room and severed all communication with friends and family. In January 1961, Bobbie and Betty were committed to the Broughton State Mental Hospital in Morgantown and were diagnosed as schizophrenics. For a full year the girls were kept on drugs and under intense psychiatric care. But no one could penetrate their private world. In 1962, the doctors separated the sisters, placing them in different wings of the institution. They were to have no contact with each other. The doctors hoped that physical isolation might shatter the strange bond between the sisters.

For a few weeks it looked as if this might occur. Then one spring evening Bobbie had a catatonic seizure. Shortly after midnight, the head nurse found her dead. Aware of the unusual affinity between the two girls, she feared the worst for Betty Jo and telephoned her ward. Betty Jo was discovered lying on the floor, dead. Both girls were curled up in a fetal position, both on their right side.

Dr. John C. Reece of the North Carolina Pathological Society performed autopsies and ruled out the possibility of suicide. Leaving the cause of death on their certificates blank, he said, "I found no demonstrable evidence of injury or disease that could cause death." In life Betty Jo had always followed her sister, and so she did in death. Psychical researchers who investigated the case were forced to conclude that the first death, Bobbie Jean's, was sensed by her sister, who then gave up her own will to live.

The sisters from North Carolina are not unique. At the Jefferson Medical College in Philadelphia, Dr.

Thomas Duane, chief of ophthalmology, and Dr. Thomas Behrendt have studied the brainwave patterns of many identical twins. Each member of a pair is placed in a different room and both twins are wired to EEGs. Duane reported in the magazine *Science* that when one twin entered an alpha brainwave state (twelve to eight cycles per second), the brainwaves of the twin in the distant room automatically switched to the same mode. This brainwave sympathy occurred even when the twins were placed on separate floors of the building. There was no specific telepathic message that one member of a pair sent to his mate; the synchronous pattern occurred quite naturally at a subconscious level. The researchers feel that twins may be predisposed to telepathy because of the strong similarities in their central nervous system and brain. Genetic commonalities in twins are already known to account for the simultaneous occurrence of wrinkles, gray hair, bald patches, tooth decay, and even the onset of cancer. There is even evidence that suggests that when other medical factors are taken into account twins tend to die at about the same age.

Evidence is mounting that the moment of death might not only be broadcast but that it might be forecast as well. Even months in advance. In recent years scientists have researched the possibility that there is a premonition of death long before any physical signs such as weight loss and skin pallor. One University of Chicago psychologist, after an intensive study of the psychology of aging, has found that elderly men and women show distinct psychological changes about a year before they begin their final physical decline.

Dr. Morton A. Lieberman of the Pritzker School of Medicine began his search for the psychic signs of the approach of death after he had a conversation with a nurse. She claimed that she could predict the deaths of her charges in a nursing home months ahead of time because, as she put it, "they just seemed to act differently." Dr. Lieberman was intrigued enough to investigate.

In his three-year study, Dr. Lieberman gave detailed psychological tests to eighty men and women between the ages of sixty-five and ninety-one, all of whom were free of major physical or mental illness at the time the study began. Within a year after the testing was completed, forty of the group had died. Dr. Lieberman then compared the results of their tests with those obtained from the remaining oldsters, who lived an average of three years longer.

He found that those who had died within a year had a lower level of adjustment to reality, less energy, and showed marked differences in many of the psychological tests. For example, they were poor in such "cognitive function" tests as the ability to learn pairs of unrelated words, and they were less introspective than those in the other group. "Those approaching death," Lieberman explained, "may have avoided introspection because they feared what they would see."

A self-image test—a series of statements that Dr. Lieberman's subjects selected as describing themselves —showed that the "impending diers" lacked assertiveness and aggressiveness and were more docile and dependent than the others. Finally, thirty-four of the forty subjects who died within a year showed an awareness —usually unconscious—of approaching death. When shown a series of pictures of elderly people involved in various situations and asked to describe what they signified, this group tended to describe direct accounts of death (for example, a struggle to save a person from drowning) or indirect symbols such as mysterious trips to unknown places. It appears that dying is a process far longer in duration than doctors have suspected.

Dr. Lieberman believes that the psychological changes that the men and women showed as death approached may be related to the physical process of dying. It may be, he said, "a body signal that takes on a mental expression." In some cases the patients themselves had premonitions of death. "Some told me, 'I am not going to live out this year,'" Dr. Lieberman recalled, "and they were right." For all, however, the knowledge of impending death may have been present at a subconscious level. Indeed, Dr. Lieberman suspects that if some of the "impending diers" had permitted themselves to be introspective and contemplative, they might actually have perceived death's call. It is quite possible that with appropriate training we might learn to read, months or years in advance, the moment of our own natural death.

The nurse who first interested Dr. Lieberman in studying the psychology of aging was able to read the subtle changes in the moods and behavior of her charges, though she was not aware of how she was able to accurately forecast deaths. But psychics are more attuned to these and other changes that herald death. In his autobiography, *Beyond Coincidence,* psychic Alex Tanous documented numerous instances where he accurately predicted a healthy person's death weeks or months in advance. During an aura reading, Tanous told one young woman from Gray, Maine, that she should not marry the man she had been dating: he had almost no aura. "I did not have the heart to tell her that the man was going to die," said Tanous. Weeks later the woman wrote to Tanous: "You told me, in reply to a question concerning the man I was keeping company with, that you couldn't see any future with this man for me. He was found dead Sunday morning, beside his bed, of a heart attack. Sincerely, Florence Wilson."

Another time a woman wrote to Tanous to say that her husband wasn't feeling well. "What do you see ahead for him?" she asked. "Once more," said Tanous, "I saw death. And since the woman had asked the question so directly, I decided to answer her directly.

I told her that her husband had brain cancer and would die of it." The woman later wrote to Tanous: "In regard to a prediction you made about a malignancy in my husband which you said would end his life. . . . Eight months after the prediction, my husband was dead of lung and brain cancer. Sincerely, Mrs. Elanore D. Murray, South Portland, Maine."

Hundreds of physicians and nurses have reported that they see "ghostly images," "mists," "clouds," and "colored lights" around the body of persons at the time of death. There also are much subtler harbingers of death—physical, psychological, and psychical. Drs. William Greene, Sidney Goldstein, and Arthur Moss, of Rochester, N.Y., studied the histories of patients who had died suddenly. The data indicated that the majority of these patients, all men, had been depressed for a week up to several months prior to sudden death. Writing in the *Archives of Internal Medicine*, the doctors stated that the depression might have produced hormonal changes and altered the central nervous system to actually bring about death. What caused the depression in the first place? Might the depression have been from an awareness, however peripheral, that they were going to die soon?

One fifty-five-year-old man had worked for many years at the Eastman Kodak plant in Rochester, New York, and had always been quite disorganized and irresponsible in regard to his family and his work. One summer he began putting everything in order both at home and at work. He was obsessed with this task. He felt depressed but was physically healthy, yet he double-checked his insurance policies, paid off outstanding bills, wrote to friends he had not communicated with for years, and finished up all his correspondence at the office. Shortly after all this was done, he died of a heart attack. In retrospect, his wife feels that he knew something was going to happen. Given the evidence that the doctors accumulated, it seems that the depression they observed in all their subjects did not cause death but was a consequence of perceiving their own death.

Profound depression of another sort is one of the five "stages of death" cataloged by thanatologist Dr. Elizabeth Kubler-Ross. The case of Mary Sparks, a Florida businesswoman, graphically illustrates all of Dr. Kubler-Ross's five steps.

Mary Sparks felt that she was going to die. She was not sure whether that feeling struck her before or after she first detected the lumpy mass beneath her right breast. "I just put the thought out of my mind," she told her twenty-five-year-old daughter, Kathy, shortly before her death. Mary so successfully suppressed her fear of death that for more than a year she ignored the lump, which she suspected was growing bigger. When it was eventually diagnosed malignant and a radical mastectomy failed to arrest the cancer, Mary resolved herself to die. But not all at once. She first passed through phases of "denial," "anger," "bargaining," and "depression."

Denial is the dying patient's first reaction: "No, not me!" is the typical response, said Dr. Kubler-Ross. "It allows the patient to collect himself and, with time, mobilize other, less-radical defenses."

Denial eventually leads to deep *anger:* "Why me?" A fifty-five-year-old dentist, dying of cancer, told Dr. Kubler-Ross: "An old man whom I have known ever since I was a little kid came down my street. He is eighty-two years old, and he is of no earthly use as far as we mortals can tell. And the thought hit me strongly —now why couldn't it have been old George instead of me?"

Anger is succeeded by *bargaining*—an act, often undetectable, to somehow stay execution of sentence. A difficult patient may abruptly turn cooperative; the reward he seeks for good behavior is an extension of his life.

After the bargaining phase the patient usually sinks

into profound *depression*. This stage, says Dr. Kubler-Ross, has a positive side: the patient is weighing the fearful price of death, preparing himself to accept the loss of everything and everyone he loves.

Then finally comes *acceptance,* when the condemned patient bows to his sentence. It is during this phase that some persons begin to report visions, voices, and the imagery of tunnels and bright lights recounted by individuals resuscitated from clinical death. Referring to the calm feelings she perceived about a week before she died, Mary Sparks told her daughter: "If I knew this was going to happen I would have accepted dying from the beginning and not have put up resistance and acted like a baby."

If Mary Sparks had been a patient of Dr. Kubler-Ross, she would have been told about the five stages of death. More importantly, Mary might have been assured that there is also a sixth stage—an afterlife. "I know that there is a hereafter," claimed Dr. Kubler-Ross, "beyond any shadow of a doubt." That is a powerful statement coming from one of the leading professionals in death research and a highly regarded psychiatrist. How can Dr. Kubler-Ross be so certain?

In the early 1970s, after investing a lifetime of work in thanatology, Dr. Kubler-Ross had her first OBE—one that duplicated exactly the kind of separation from the physical body that takes place at the time of clinical death. After a strenuous day of counseling eight dying patients, Dr. Kubler-Ross lay down to rest. Her OBE occurred spontaneously. Later, she was incredulous to learn from a woman who had been present in the room with her that she had appeared to be dead—without pulse or respiration. Aware of the imagery characteristic of clinical death, but poorly informed of OBE research at that time, Dr. Kubler-Ross began to read everything that had been done in that field.

Soon she visited Robert Monroe in Virginia. Dr. Kubler-Ross had read the accounts of his OBEs in

Monroe's book *Journey's Out of the Body,* and she was impressed with the testing of Monroe by Dr. Charles Tart of the University of California. Using a relaxation technique he developed himself, Monroe at that time was teaching people how to have OBEs, and Dr. Kubler-Ross caught on immediately. One night in Virginia as she was trying to sleep, Dr. Kubler-Ross had a profound experience:

> "I had one of the most incredible experiences of my life. In one sentence: I went through every single death of every single one of my thousand patients. And I mean the physical pain, the dyspnea, the agony, the screaming for help. The pain was beyond any description. There was no time to think and no time for anything except that twice I caught a breath, like between two labor pains. I was able to catch my breath for a split second, and I pleaded—I guess with God—for a shoulder to lean on, for one human shoulder, and I visualized a man's shoulder that I could put my head on.
>
> "And a thunderous voice came: 'You shall not be given.' Those words. And then I went back to my agony and doubling up in bed. But I was awake, it wasn't a dream. I was reliving every single death of every one of my dying patients."

She continued to beg for God to help her, and again the voice boomed, "You shall not be given." She raged with fury. "I have helped so many, and now no one would help me." That outburst of anger made her suddenly realize that "you have to do it alone, that no one can do it for you," and immediately her suffering vanished and was replaced by "the most incredible rebirth experience."

Rebirth experiences have been reported by mystics, psychics, and ordinary people, but perhaps never before by a person of Dr. Kubler-Ross's experience and

69

special training. She is an astute observer and it's worth considering her adventure in detail as she told it to Ann Nietzke of *Human Behavior*. Light, we will see, plays a major role in Dr. Kubler-Ross's rebirth.

"It was so beautiful there are no words to describe it. It started with my belly wall vibrating, and I looked—this was full, open eyes, fully conscious—and I said, 'This can't be,' I mean, anatomically, physiologically, it was not possible. It vibrated very fast. And then everywhere I looked in the room—my legs, the closet, the window—everything started to vibrate into a million molecules. Everything vibrated at this incredible speed. And in front of me was a form. The closest way to describe it was like a vagina. I looked at that, and as I focused on it, it turned into a lotus flower bud. And while I watched this in utter amazement—there were incredibly beautiful colors and smells and sounds in the room—it opened up into the most beautiful lotus flower.

"Behind it was a sunrise, the brightest light you can imagine without hurting your eyes. And as the flower opened, its absolute fullness in this life was totally present. At that moment the light was full and open, like the whole sun was there, and the flower was full and open. The vibrations stopped, and the million molecules, including me—it was all part of the world—fell into one piece. It was like a million pieces fell into one, and I was part of that one. And I finally thought, 'I'm okay, because I'm part of all this.' "

Later, Dr. Kubler-Ross added: "I know that's a crazy description for anybody who has not experienced this. It is the closest I can share it with you. It was so incredibly beautiful that if I would describe it as a thousand orgasms at one time, it would be a very shabby comparison. There are no words for it, really. We have very inadequate language."

So profound was Dr. Kubler-Ross's experience that it took months for her to get over it.

"The next morning as I walked outside, it was incredible, because I was in love with every leaf, every bird—even the pebbles. I know I didn't walk on the pebbles but a little above them. And I kept saying to the pebbles, 'I can't step on you because I can't hurt you.' They were as alive as I was, and I was part of this whole alive universe. It took me months to be able to describe all this in any halfway adequate words."

Dr. Kubler-Ross's experience with what mystics call "cosmic consciousness" only suggested to her that there could be an afterlife, that there was a continuity among all things not only in space but also in time. One of the things that finally convinced her of the existence of a hereafter was a visit to her office by a former patient of hers, Mrs. Schwartz—after Mrs. Schwartz's death and burial. As Dr. Kubler-Ross related her own Death Encounter of the Fourth Kind, Mrs. Schwartz appeared as her fully human self to thank the doctor for having taken care of her and to encourage her to continue her work with dying patients. At first Dr. Kubler-Ross thought that she was hallucinating, but when the figure persisted, she demanded that Mrs. Schwartz write a note and sign it. The note is now in the possession of a priest who had also worked with Mrs. Schwartz and who verified the handwriting.

Since then Dr. Kubler-Ross has seen other deceased patients and has even tape-recorded the voice of one, Willie. "I understand that this is very far out," Dr. Kubler-Ross admitted, "and I don't want people to be less skeptical, really. I am skeptical myself. The scientist in me needed Mrs. Schwartz to sign a paper, though

I knew she was in my office. And I needed a tape-recording of Willie's voice. I still listen to it and think sometimes it's one big, incredible dream. I am still filled with this incredible sense of awe and miracle."

For coming forward and telling the world what she has experienced, many of Dr. Kubler-Ross's colleagues, who at one time revered her as a leader in their field, have turned against her. But Dr. Kubler-Ross holds fast to her belief in survival. Her experience of the continuity of space, time, and matter matches perfectly what psychical researcher Dean W. R. Matthews has suggested as a working definition of survival. His hypothesis, which seems to make sense biologically, is "that the center of consciousness which was in existence before death does not cease to be in existence after death, and that the experience of this center after death has the same kind of continuity with its experience before death as that of a man who sleeps for a while and wakes again."

Now we are about to see that some of the best evidence for survival of bodily death comes from Death Encounters of the Fourth Kind.

5

Death Encounters of the Fourth Kind

These are spectacular manifestations. They offer proof of survival—that is, if you accept the evidence. And there is fairly weighty evidence that the dead can contact the living. And vice versa.

Death Encounters of the Fourth Kind can occur in a variety of ways: parasensory hearing, where a living person hears the voice of a person who is clinically dead or just plain dead; parasensory vision, where a person sees the image of someone who is undergoing the process of death or who has already died; and parasensory touch, in which a person feels a cool breath on his cheek or a gentle tapping on his arm or shoulder from the temporarily or the permanently deceased. All these phenomena have been documented. We will examine all the evidence currently available; for contact with the dead clearly implies the existence of an afterlife.

Jeff Barker is a fifty-five-year-old engineer for a TV station in the Midwest. He suffers from an ailment in which his body does not produce sufficient blood, and he regularly needs transfusions to stay alive. In February 1977, Jeff Barker waited too long for his transfusion and went into shock. He was rushed to a local hospital, unconscious, at about 10:30 P.M. on a Friday. No one except his immediate family knew of his hospitalization or that he was near death.

Eighteen miles away, Sheila Nolan, a technical director for ABC, took her late evening coffee break. She was passing from the lounge to the ladies' room on the fourth floor when she sensed someone else in the corridor. She looked up and saw Jeff Barker. The image startled her. First, he was not supposed to be on duty that night; second, after blinking her eyes, she realized that his figure was a ghost. Aside from natural fear, she was mystified by the fact that he was wearing a green hospital gown covered in one area with purple dots. The apparition vanished as quickly as it had appeared and Sheila tried to forget all about it. She had been tired and had been working long, exhausting hours lately. Undoubtedly she had hallucinated.

Jeff eventually regained consciousness, and a few days later, back at his job, he discussed his experience with a coworker. While unconscious he had traveled out of his body. Instead of going home to his worried family, he found himself, "by force of habit," he said, at the television studio. He had not seen Sheila, but it was not long before she learned of his strange tale and confided her own to him. At first Jeff discounted her story, but when she described his hospital gown and the purple marks on it, he was convinced that she had seen him. The marks, Jeff knew from past experience, were from blood that had splattered during the transfusion and turned purple against the green gown.

It is rare enough for one person to see or hear an astral body, but rarer still if three people independently see the same spirit. Molly Childs, age twenty-six, works in California with psychologist Dr. Charles Garfield, counseling dying patients. She is familiar with the death experiences of others, and in a 1972 motorcycle acci-

dent Molly had her own brush with death. It proved
to be a Death Encounter of the First Kind, beautiful
but purely subjective. Four years later her grandmother
died. Despite her familiarity with dying, Molly was hit
hard by the death. One morning shortly after her
grandmother's funeral, Molly was seated in her living
room:

"All of a sudden I knew Grandmother was there
in the room. I knew she was there and I carried
on a conversation with her. Not out loud, just in
my head. And she answered. It's hard to explain.
The best I can do is say that we communicated by
feelings, as you might do in the presence of a person you're emotionally very close to—talking without words, just sensing feelings. My grandmother
was really there, and all this went on for about
fifteen minutes."

At first Molly thought her longing for her grandmother had manifested itself in a delusion, albeit a
very cogent one. But a few days after her experience
she received separate letters from her two sisters. Each
claimed that she had the distinct feeling of being
visited by their grandmother. The sensations were so
strong that both sisters were frightened and had felt
the need to confide in Molly. After they discussed their
individual visitations, they had to conclude that their
grandmother had truly been present in each of their
homes—on the same day, in different parts of the state.
"I have read that after a person dies," said Molly,
"their astral body can hang around and visit people
who were important to them in life, try to make
contact. I believe that this is what my grandmother
did."

Despite the number of death apparitions seen by
people—even multiple sightings as in the case of Molly
Childs and her sisters—scientists demand more con-

crete proof of contact with the dead. If an entity as ephemeral as an astral body can be seen by human eyes and heard by human ears, it is possible that the voices of the deceased can be tape-recorded and their images photographed. This is the rationale offered by researchers who try to use modern photographic and tape-recording equipment to prove contact with the dead. By their own accounts, they have had amazingly good results, considering the complexity of their task.

Such work has roots in the birth of electronics. Following the advent of every new mode of communications there comes a flurry of excitement and claims in psychic circles that this most recent electronics breakthrough makes it possible to receive messages from beyond the grave. In the early part of this century there were a few incidents where a telegraph spontaneously rattled out a Morse code alert to a future disaster, and with the invention of the telephone came several claims that deceased relatives could be heard speaking in the static that then dominated most calls. Radio too allegedly brought messages from the dead, and the phenomenon of automatic writing got a big boost with the advent of the electric typewriter. But the most impressive spirit messages, according to many psychical researchers, have for the last fifteen years been captured on tape-recorders. Since the methods employed are easy, an increasing number of researchers and laymen have attempted, often successfully, to pick up unidentifiable voices on blank tape. In some cases, rigorous experimental conditions have precluded the possibility that the voices were merely extraneous pickups from radio and television broadcasts. Are we to believe that they are actually voices of the dead?

It all began in 1959 when Friedrich Jurgenson, a painter and operatic tenor, was recording bird calls in a forest area near his home in Mölndal, Sweden. On playback, among the twitterings and chirpings Jurgenson heard a resonant male voice saying in Norwegian something about "nocturnal bird songs" or "bird voices of the night." Jurgenson was fascinated enough to make more bird recordings, and invariably he found human voices, sometimes that of his deceased mother, warning, "Friedrich, you are being watched!" "When I received the voice of my mother," said the septuagenarian Jurgenson, "I was convinced that I had made an important discovery." At an international press conference Jurgenson played his tapes and in 1964 he published a book in Swedish, titled *Voices from the Universe*, which covered his four years of studying the voice phenomenon. His second book, *Radio Contact with the Dead*, published in 1967, was translated into German and was eventually read by Latvian psychologist Dr. Konstantin Raudive. Excited by the prospect of contacting the dead, but duly skeptical, the late Dr. Raudive visited Jurgenson and learned his recording methods. He soon improved on them, and with his own messages, which were astonishingly clear, he catapulted the voice phenomenon to worldwide attention with his book *Breakthrough*, which gave parts of his messages from more than twenty-seven thousand different voices. In the United States and England the taped voices became known as Raudive voices, and electronics engineers, scientists, and psychics put Raudive through some grueling tests in an attempt to discover the source of his voices.

Raudive never doubted that he was hearing from the dead, because so many of his voices identified themselves by name and declared themselves to be in other dimensions of existence. As is true with the voices being recorded on more sophisticated equipment today, Raudive's voices differed widely from ordinary human speech in pitch, amplitude, and intensity. And their soft, irregular rhythms often came in peculiar cadences. Raudive said of this: 'The sentence construction obeys rules that differ radically from those of ordinary speech, and although the voices seem to speak in the same way as we do, the anatomy of their speech apparatus must be different from our own."

The fact that the voices are audible to us and that we can understand the speech, albeit with difficulty sometimes, confirms that they exist physically and independently from us, Raudive believed. For him, the purpose of studying the voices was not to expound religious interpretations, not to philosophize, but to arrive at empirical results that could be verified under rigorous test conditions. And the most rigorous test came shortly before Raudive's death.

Many reputable scientists and electronics experts had analyzed the thousands of tapes that Raudive prepared. There was no question in anyone's mind that sounds were there—only their source was open to doubt. Most engineers felt certain that the voices were extraneous radio and television pickups. In order to solve the mystery, in March 1971, several scientists decided to tape Raudive's voice in a recording studio. Engineers installed special equipment to block out any chance of interference from radio and television broadcasts; the best equipment available was used, with high-quality magnetic tapes. Raudive used one tape-recorder, while another, electronically linked up and synchronized with the first, served as a control. Raudive was not allowed to touch so much as a dial; all he had to do was talk into a microphone. A third tape-recorder, synchronized to Raudive's, monitored every sound in the studio. For eighteen minutes Raudive's voice was taped, and no one present heard any unusual sounds. But on playing back the tape, the scientists found over one hundred voices on it—some of which were so clear that they did not require amplification.

The electronics experts were dumbfounded. What's more, the control tape-recorder, which should have picked up exactly what Raudive's machine did, was completely blank. "This was electronically impossible," recalled the British engineer who headed the test.

Raudive's tapes continue to be analyzed today. The messages are not profound in content. Quite the contrary. A female voice, for example, says in Latvian, "Kostulit, this is your mother." Or it may claim to be his sister Tekle, his cousin Mona, his aunt, or a notable such as Goethe or Hitler. Usually they merely identify themselves; only occasionally is there a sentence such as: *"Tu no naves dzirdi!"* (Latvian for, "You hear from the realm of the dead"); or *"Te mirusiem, mes ivojam,"* (Latvian for, "Here are the dead, we live"). Perhaps the most significant communication Raudive received, out of almost 100,000 recordings, was a female voice saying in Latvian, "There is no death here. The earth is death."

Raudive is dead, but the Reverend Betty Dye of Stonewall, Georgia, a minister and psychic healer, who began making voice tapes in 1972, claims to have contacted Raudive on the evening of April 16, 1976—and many nights thereafter. Dye's tapes have not yet been studied by experts, but clearly audible on the tapes is a male voice who identifies himself as Dr. Raudive. In fragmentary sentences, the voice encourages further investigation of the voice phenomenon and stresses that there are many spirits who want to make contact with the living.

Raudive died believing that, as he said, "My discovery may be too big to be believable." But others have had success in making recordings and have received more-meaningful messages.

The clearest and most meaningful voices recorded so far have come from Joseph and Michael Lamoreaux of Washington State. They work with a $13.88 recorder. Experts have studied the voices and the Lamoreauxes' recording methods, and they conclude that no trickery is involved in making the tapes. The voices are genuinely from an unknown source—they identify themselves as existing beyond the grave. Some of the words used by the voices are of an arcane Anglo-European origin known only to specialized linguists, and therefore they could not have been made up by the brothers.

Michael Lamoreaux, a teacher living in Kittitas, Washington, began taping in October 1972, after he had read Raudive's book *Breakthrough*. After two months with no results, he went to visit his elder brother, Joe, who had worked as a radio-signal interceptor for the Air Force. Joe recorded voices the very first time he tried. That first transmission was very distorted, but said Mike, "It sent us on our way."

Joseph Lamoreaux told us that initially the voices he and his brother picked up were whispers, almost inaudible. Joe found that he could decipher the sounds better than Mike could, and they began to spend most of their time making and listening to tapes.

They found, as Raudive and Jurgenson had, that practice at listening to the voices was essential if they were to recognize what was being said. On a typical day, after about ten hours of taping, the brothers had about fifteen minutes of tape voices out of hundreds of feet of tape. It was not until Joe's ear became acutely tuned to the soft hum that he realized that the particular voices they were receiving were continuous—every inch of tape was packed. There was not a single pause, not even overlaps. The Lamoreauxes were getting the most extensive transmissions anyone had ever recorded.

"We learned," said Joseph Lamoreaux, "that occasionally when a recording is being made using the microphone, the voice entities are sometimes able to alter or modulate audible noises or sounds in the room into speech patterns. Richard Sheargold of England refers to these voices as 'modulated noise.' Most experimenters sooner or later find this to be true. And the voice entities have confirmed that they are sometimes able to do this. They say they 'use the waves.'" Some researchers believe that it is easier for the spirits to use energy that is already in the room, and to shape it into their own words, than to try to muster the energy themselves.

The Lamoreaux brothers have developed a method in which they ask a question of the communicating spirits, let the tape-recorder run fifteen to twenty seconds, play it back many times until they are reasonably sure what is said, and then write it down. They now have over a hundred transcripts and thousands of responses, all catalogued, and they have kept all their recordings. Mike recently told psychic investigator Susy Smith, who wrote about the brothers in her book *Voices of the Dead?*, "We often don't receive clear answers to all our questions, but we have received much information. The entities have told us about the different planes of existence where they live, and they have explained how their voices are transmitted to us."

The names of the eight planes of existence, written down phonetically by the Lamoreaux brothers, sound comical until one realizes that they have ancient origins. Professor Donald Cummings of Central Washington State College, a linguist, became so fascinated by the sounds of the names that he did research into their background. He found that they have Anglo-European roots that are quite appropriate for the planes they represent. The planes are:

Pareenah. The name of the earth planes of existence where we are now living. The inhabitants of this plane are called *man*. The roots of this word, as researched by Professor Cummings, reveal that it is the "starting place" or "beginning."

Deenah. The name for the first plane of existence after death. This is the plane inhabited by those who normally communicate with us. The

DEATH ENCOUNTERS

root means the "God place" or the "place of the gods or deities."

Ree. Another plane on the same level as Deenah, but spatially separate from it. Whereas Deenah is more formal and "spiritual," Ree seems to be more "physical," more within reach. After death, those having adjustment problems in Deenah are sent to Ree. It may also be the plane to which the astral body travels in OBEs, and where it hovers during clinical death. The root means to "do over, repeat." This could explain why many survivors of clinical death report that they came back to "do over" again, or emendate their lives.

Nilow. A place considered quite low, almost as low as Pareenah. Those who do not adjust are sent to Nilow until they can function properly in the higher planes. Both *ni* and *low* are roots, meaning "lower" or "below."

Ultareenah. Up from Ree, literally. A place where there is healing. Doctors are there to help those who need to adjust. The inhabitants of Ultareenah are the "spirit doctors" who do psychic healing or faith healing to help us here in the physical plane. When a human healer shifts his state of consciousness, it is believed that he is unknowingly putting himself in contact with the "spirit doctors" on Ultareenah and receiving their advice. The word translates as the "ultimate Ree place," and it is the highest place one can progress to from Ree.

Montayloo. Directly above Deenah, it is the place to which Deenah's inhabitants, the Moozla, progress when they are ready. *Mont* is the root of words like "mount" and "mountain." It means a place higher than Deenah.

Piloncentric. A very high place that the Lamoreauxes have not been able to learn much about. If "pilon" is spelled "pylon," it translates to "tower."

82

Metanah. The highest plane of which the communicants have knowledge, yet perhaps not the highest plane there is. Many of the great religious leaders are said to live there. (People on the other planes have to have special devices in order to communicate with people on earth. These devices —described as "machines"—are called the *domnit* and the *lens* by the spirit voices. The domnit is what is used in order to communicate through mediums. The domnit and the lens used together allow communication via tape-recorders. It is possible that spirits on higher planes are on an entirely different level of existence, one in which they cannot, or perhaps do not, wish to communicate with earthlings.)

The Lamoreaux brothers offer their messages to anyone interested in survival research. They are particularly interested in having more scientists and linguists analyze the tapes. They realize that many people are horrified or even repulsed by the rather mundane messages, and by such a seemingly analytical hierarchy existing in the hereafter. Does the afterlife really have "levels of society" too?

Despite the Lamoreaux brothers' optimistic evaluation of the voice phenomenon, much controversy rages over it. The voices get through even when sophisticated filtering and shielding equipment is used, but that has not convinced all skeptics. Some scientists argue that the voices are not from the dead but are the experimenters' own subconscious thoughts psychokinetically spilling themselves onto tape. To some people, direct communications from the subconscious mind seem vastly more feasible, and more comforting, than Raudive's and the Lamoreauxes' theory that the voices are from discarnate entities.

Analysis of the voice phenomenon shows that the best results are obtained by people who are emotionally involved in the proceedings. Those who desperately want to contact someone who has died, and those who most strongly deny the reality of the voices, tend to be the ones favored with the apparently personal communications. To record voices, a tape must be run through a machine. Nothing has ever been found impressed directly onto a stationary tape, and no recordings of voices have ever been made by a machine that ran in an empty room. People must be present. While they are, of course, the possibility always remains that they could unconsciously be responsible for the voices.

Perhaps the strongest argument in favor of a supernatural source of the voices is the fact that some of them speak in languages unknown to anyone present at the time they were recorded. This is strengthened by the fact that some of the voices give information that is known to no one present, and, on later checking, it proves to be correct. One fact about the voice phenomenon is clear: living people must be present for the voices to be recorded. Perhaps they serve as a catalyst, a sort of medium through which the spirits anchor themselves to this world for a short period of time. This is a popular theory among many psychical researchers and virtually all the people who report getting the voices.

If Death Encounters of the Fourth Kind can be captured on tape, it is not surprising that they also can be recorded on film. Psychic photography, also called "thought photography," involves the ability to transfer images that exist in a person's mind, or beyond the grave, onto conventional film. It is a small branch of parapsychology because there are not many psychics who claim to possess this talent. One who does make that claim is the thirty-two-year-old Israeli, Uri Geller, best known for his ability to psychokinetically bend spoons, keys, and other metal objects. On rare occasions Geller has produced thought photographs.

Lawrence Fried, an award-winning photographer and a former president of the American Society of Photographers in Communications, has documented such an event with Geller. Holding Fried's Nikon camera in his hand, with the lens cap taped on securely, Geller successfully "exposed" an entire roll of film, which, when developed, revealed images of him on several frames. But Geller has not produced images of the dead—though he believes that this is possible. He said, "If something as nonmaterial as thoughts can be projected through space to people, and captured on film, then I don't see why, through a living agent, a dead person's image cannot be photographed."

Ted Serios, the psychic photographer who has been studied by Dr. Julie Eisenbud, a psychiatrist from the University of Colorado, dealt almost exclusively in photographing the dead before his talent waned a few years ago. Serios produced hundreds of pictures of his deceased relatives and friends, and many unidentifiable spirits. They all appeared in hazy, slightly blurred white images, usually surrounded by a mist, that resembles a diffuse and glaring aura. Dr. Eisenbud told us that the best current psychic photographers of "curious images" (which in many cases have been identified as images of dead people from present and historical times) are the members of the Veilleux family of Sidney, Maine.

Many of the members of the Veilleux family have the ability to take psychic photographs, but it is the sixty-five-year-old father, Joseph, and his two sons, Fred, age thirty-five, and Richard, age thirty-one, who are the best and most consistent at it. They use an ordinary Polaroid camera and black-and-white film. Their startling photographic effects include globes of light, mysterious clouds, scenery not in view of the camera, and, most striking, clear faces of people known to be dead. Dr. Eisenbud began to study the Veilleuxes in 1968 and he is convinced that their photographs are genuine—he feels certain that he has proof that images from beyond the grave can be captured on film. The Veilleuxes have also been studied at the Human Dimensions Institute of Rosary Hill College in Buffalo, New York, by biochemist Dr. Justa Smith, and observed taking their psychic pictures by Charles Honorton, former president of the Parapsychological Association. Everyone who has seen Joseph, Fred, and Richard take photographs agrees that something highly unusual, and very genuine, is taking place.

The Veilleuxes began experimenting with a Ouija board in 1965, but they seem to have inherited their abilities from a long line of psychic ancestors. Perhaps it is more than coincidental that Joseph, who lays concrete at construction sites, also works part-time as a caretaker for several cemeteries in his hometown. Both his sons are masons by trade, but during slack seasons they too have helped out in cemeteries.

The Veilleuxes are occasionally told when and where to take pictures by instructions from their Ouija board. For example, on January 19, 1969, the Veilleuxes were communicating, via Ouija board, with an entity who introduced herself as Carol Farnham. "What proof can you offer us as to your authenticity?" they asked her. "A circle of light in a transparency is all I can offer," she answered. "Are you speaking of a paranormal photograph?" Joseph asked. She answered yes and gave instructions. Joseph fetched his Polaroid camera, aimed it at the east wall of the kitchen, and snapped the shutter. The picture slowly developed into a brilliant circle of light.

Joseph implored the entity for more information. Over the next few days the Ouija board spelled out the details of Carol Farnham's violent death in the Hotel Shamrock on Kansas Street in San Diego, California. It also gave a number of names and addresses in New Hampshire, Connecticut, New Foundland, and California, where Carol Farnham had said information could be gained about her mother. The Veilleuxes investigated and found some of the names factual.

From that point on, other entities identified themselves and told Joseph, Fred, or Richard where in their kitchen to aim their Polaroid to get "curious" pictures. At other times, the Veilleuxes simply aimed at random and came up with images of dead people. Their work parallels that of the traditional nineteenth-century "spirit photographers" in that the Veilleuxes exert no conscious volition for the pictures to be produced and they do not feel that they are in control of the images they receive. While the Veilleuxes take pictures they experience cool breezes across their faces and hear noises in other rooms of their house.

In late 1969 the Veilleuxes went to Denver to visit Dr. Eisenbud and to be studied. Dr. Eisenbud took the Veilleux men to various local cemeteries and let them snap pictures at random of tombstones, trees, and sky. He carefully supervised their every move. Many pictures, Dr. Eisenbud told us, contained clear images of people surrounded by auras. On further investigation Dr. Eisenbud was surprised to find that the faces were easily identified as those of people who were dead—in fact, some pictures were clear images of men who had died more than a hundred years ago. Dr. Eisenbud rules out trickery in many instances because the only known pictures of some of these people are in the Noah Rose collection at the University of Oklahoma's Western History Department. A fact that the Veilleuxes did not know. And they have never been to Oklahoma. Nor has anyone ever borrowed the pictures from the collection.

On their second trip to Denver, Dr. Eisenbud took the Veilleux men to the office of the Medical Photography Department of the University of Colorado Medical School. The chairman of the department had died just a few days before. They went into the dead man's office and one of the Veilleuxes shot three Polaroid pictures of the empty desk. Two of the pictures turned out blank. But one, Dr. Eisenbud claimed, was the beginning of a milky white image—it was light and faint, but unmistakably the image of a man. The new chairman of the photography department, who was present, came away flabbergasted.

The Veilleuxes have even tried to take psychic pictures of the surface of the moon. In 1968 Dr. Eisenbud received a phone call from William Cook, a scientist at North American Rockwell Corporation in Los Angeles, who had prepared all the photography experiments for the *Apollo 8* space flight. A parapsychology buff, Cook wanted Dr. Eisenbud to arrange an attempt to take psychic photographs of the surface of the moon before the first spacecraft, *Apollo 8*, landed. He would then compare the two sets of photographs. Dr. Eisenbud asked the Veilleuxes and they agreed to try, but they warned, "You know we can't hit on specific targets; these things just happen." One evening at home, the Veilleuxes concentrated on the moon and continued to click their camera, aimed all the while at the kitchen wall. Several pictures developed strange images and these were sent to Cook three days before *Apollo 8* landed on the moon. Cook said, "The pictures are unlike any terrain in Maine, or the United States." He claimed that they looked amazingly like the later *Apollo* images of the surface of the moon, showing craters, canals, and rough, dry, badly pockmarked terrain.

Dr. Eisenbud said of the Veilleuxes: "My impressions of them are totally favorable. I have absolutely no reason to believe there is any fraud or deception involved. They seem able to photograph images of the deceased."

What the Veilleuxes feel is photographic proof of an afterlife, they back up with their tape-recordings of voices from beyond the grave. Some of the voices claim to belong to the people in the paranormal photographs taken by the family, and one of their first recorded messages, which came after a camera session, was: "We are trying to make contact." Since then, the brothers have even taken a portable tape-recorder into some local cemeteries, but the voices they recorded there were about as faint as the ones they now get at home. They had expected to get better voices at the cemeteries.

Many researchers have listened to the taped voices and studied the spirit photographs and admit that "something" is present, but they are unwilling to believe that that something is generated by spirits. Dr. Andrija Puharich, the New York physician who brought Uri Geller to the United States, believes that the voices might be those of extraterrestrial beings trying to make contact with us. This, he thinks, could account for the poor quality of the communications. Others insist that the voices and images are psychokinetic manifestations from our own minds: we project onto tape and film thoughts of people whom we know have died. Dr. Eisenbud offered this statement: "The important point to make, I think, is that paranormally putting voices on tape or images on film is essentially no more mysterious than telepathically putting images into the mind or telekinetically initiating an action. Telepathy and metal-bending are just witnessed more often."

While telepathy and telekinesis (or psychokinesis) violate the tenets of science, for many people, voices and images of the dead violate one of the basic premises of Western religion: that there can be no contact between the living and the dead. But the assumption that the dead forever rest in peace, and silence, on closer examination seems false. Throughout history, religious literature is filled with instances of images and voices coming in revelations to saints and to ordinary people. Consequently, some people believe that paranormal tape-recordings and photographs made with electronic equipment are merely a modern-day version of the spirit revelations of old. "In the past," said one researcher, "spirits spoke directly to a saint or appeared in front of him. Today, it's the psychic who records the spirit's voice on tape or his image on film." Really, is one manifestation any more mysterious than the other? To be completely honest, we would have to say that revelations in the past were a lot more subjective than the revelations witnessed today. For there is no way that a saint's vision can be scientifically studied, but evidence on tapes and films can be rigorously scrutinized over and over again. This is the merit of Death Encounters of the Fourth Kind.

PART II

6

The American Book of the Dead or Learning How to Die

When you know that an event is going to occur, you prepare for it. This is true if you are about to get married, to have a baby, or to send a child to college. If you're about to make a journey, you certainly plan, making sure that reservations are in order and that you have the proper clothing for the climate. Ironically, most people make no preparation for the most important and inevitable journey in their life: death.

We are not speaking of such things as preparing a will, purchasing a cemetery plot, or setting one's finances in order (though lack of preparation is also evident in these areas). We mean planning for the physical and spiritual event of death itself. What might dying feel like? What sights and sounds might you experience as the moment of death approaches? And when that moment does arrive, will you be psychologically prepared to see "take away" figures, to glimpse spirits of a deceased mother or father, or to enter a tunnel with a light at the end? Whether you view these things as harbingers of a hereafter or merely as hallucinations of a dying brain, either way, it would be comforting to know what to expect. It is the lack of this kind of planning that lies at the root of the almost inordinate fear of dying that is experienced by most Westerners. (In Eastern and African cultures, where they make elaborate preparations for death and school the dying in what they can expect, people do not know the concept of thanatophobia.)

Fortunately, this situation is beginning to change in the United States. From texts such as the *Tibetan Book of the Dead*—which literally is a manual for dying—and from the tales of people revived from clinical death, theologians and scientists are beginning to piece together a sort of manual that might one day be called the American Book of the Dead.

Two pioneers in this area are Drs. Stanislav Grof and Joan Halifax. In the 1960s they began giving the hallucinogen LSD to terminally ill cancer patients. By altering a patient's state of consciousness, Drs. Grof and Halifax were able to greatly relieve the physical pain that accompanies the last stages of cancer. In doing so, they got more than they had bargained for: dying patients who had received LSD reported hallucinations strikingly similar to the events related by people revived from clinical death. Was there a real connection? LSD was instrumental in relieving pain because it let the patient feel "detached from his body," sort of precipitating an OBE. Was this a genuine OBE, a mini-death that permitted a patient to glimpse what he might expect from death? Suspecting that this might be the case, Drs. Grof and Halifax augmented their LSD treatments by instructing patients in what dying might be like. Dean, a twenty-six-year-old black man, provided an enlightening case of their work.

Dean had advanced cancer of the colon when he began psychedelic therapy. Several years earlier, one of his kidneys had been removed because it was malignant. When Dr. Stanislav Grof first met Dean, the ureter from his remaining kidney had become obstructed by infection and Dean was being poisoned by his own waste. With Dean's permission, Dr. Grof immediately began LSD therapy. After eight days of progressively worsening uremia, one evening Dr. Grof received an urgent call from Dean's wife, Flora. Arriving at the hospital, Dr. Grof found Dean semiconscious. Several relatives tried to maintain verbal contact with him, but it was clear to Dr. Grof that Dean was near death. Soon he slipped into a coma.

Dr. Joan Halifax had accompanied Dr. Grof to the hospital that night, and she sat by Dean's bed and began to read to him from the Bordo Thodol, using her own Westernized version of this Eastern manual for dying. That Dean was comatose made no difference to her; she took a gamble that he might still be able to hear her. In essence, Dr. Halifax suggested that Dean move toward any light he might see, and that he attempt to merge with it, unafraid of its splendor. Death was inevitable and Dr. Halifax was instructing Dean on how to die, trying to make it easier for him. However, the surgical team suddenly decided to operate, in a final attempt to save Dean's life. Dr. Halifax continued to read to Dean while he was being prepared for surgery. During the operation, which was long and difficult, Dean suffered *two* cardiac arrests that resulted in clinical death, and he was resuscitated on both occasions.

Later, in the intensive care unit, Dean looked at Dr. Halifax and said, "You changed your dress." Unwilling to believe that somebody who had been comatose first observed, then remembered, such a subtlety, Dr. Grof started to question Dean. It soon became obvious that while in a coma Dean had correctly perceived the people present in his room and was able to remember bits of their conversations. He even noted, though his eyes had been closed, that at one point Dr. Halifax had tears running down her cheeks.

While part of Dean's consciousness had observed his surroundings, another part heard Dr. Halifax talking about the light. At first he had seen only a black void, but then he found the light, floated toward it, unafraid, and felt that he actually fused with it. Her words, Dean said, had comforted him and helped him find the light. While all this had been going on, another part of Dean's consciousness saw a movie on the ceiling of the hospital room. As Dean later described it, the movie was a vivid reenactment of all the bad things he had done in his life. He saw a gallery of faces of all the people whom he had killed in the Korean War and all the youngsters he had beaten up as an adolescent hoodlum. He said he suffered the pain and agony of all the people whom he had hurt during his lifetime. While all this was in progress, Dean was also aware of the "presence of God," watching and judging the film of Dean's life.

Dean had more to tell. He had undergone Dr. Grof's LSD therapy, he had almost died naturally in his hospital bed, and he had experienced clinical death twice during his operation. Dean found all four experiences amazingly similar, and he thanked Drs. Grof and Halifax for their LSD treatments, which had prepared him, he said, for what he had actually encountered at death's door. Dean commented: "Without the sessions [LSD], I would have been terribly scared by what was happening, but, knowing these states, I was not afraid at all." Dean had seen the void, the tunnel, the light, and spirits, and he had, he said, heard the voice of God. Soon after his surgery he died. We can only imagine that his final death did not frighten him but filled him with awe, and that he accepted it graciously and willingly.

Dr. Grof is a scientist and he realizes that the imagery that accompanies death can be triggered by a wide range of processes: a variety of psychedelic substances, sensory isolation or bombardment, monotonous chanting, extreme sleep deprivation, severe fasting, and various meditation techniques and spiritual practices. Also, severe injuries, stress, shock, and certain mental disorders such as psychosis (particularly schizophrenia and melancholia) can cause a person to hallucinate a void and blinding lights and hear strange voices and "celestial" music. Indeed, it seems that whenever the human brain is forced into an extreme condition, the "imagery of death" is a natural consequence.

Many cultures make use of this fact in their religious rituals in order to induce transcendent or spiritual experiences. Indians use periods of hyperventilation alternating with prolonged withholding of breath; other Easterners obstruct the larynx by twisting the tongue backward, or directly constrict the carotid arteries by prolonged hanging by the feet, with the ensuing congestion of blood in the head and brain producing anoxia. Taoists advocate a technique of breathing during meditation in which the intake of air is so slow that a tiny feather placed in front of the nostrils remains still. In fact, some of the earliest forms of baptism involved holding a person's head under water until he almost drowned. When his lungs ached and his blood and brain were near the point of oxygen starvation, he was permitted to surface. The person had been near death, and, not surprisingly, he saw his baptism as the rebirth that it was meant to signify. Its Eastern counterpart is a practice in which a guru holds his disciple's head under water for an excessive period of time and lets him surface only after repeated distress signals. While the disciple, blue in the face, his eyes bulging, gasps for breath, the guru asks, "Do you want knowledge or air?" A serious-minded disciple is expected to opt for knowledge, at which time he is resubmerged. Some philosophers believe that mankind's earliest concepts of spirituality and an afterlife are based on reports of individuals who had such death-rebirth experiences.

There are many ways to part the golden curtain and glimpse the next realm. Transcendence, we know, plays a critical role in all death encounters. Just as the techniques of Drs. Grof and Halifax may one day be part of our American Book of the Dead, so too may the observations of psychiatrist Russell Noyes of the University of Iowa Medical School. Dr. Noyes has made a lengthy study of sudden near-death cases. His unique subjects include individuals who were unconscious from near-drowning and were revived; fire victims who leaped from skyscrapers; some nearly successful suicides; mountain climbers who plummeted hundreds of feet and landed on a blanket of snow with only minor injuries; and survivors of airplane disasters and skydiving accidents such as the one experienced by nineteen-year-old Bob Hall. In December 1972, Hall jumped from a plane thirty-three hundred feet above the Coolidge, Arizona, airport; his parachute did not open and he hit the ground at an estimated sixty miles per hour. Miraculously, he survived. A few days later, recovering from nothing more serious than a smashed nose and loosened teeth, he told reporters what the plunge had been like:

"I screamed. I knew I was dead and that my life was ended. All my past life flashed before my eyes, it really did. I saw my mother's face, all the homes I've lived in, the military academy I attended, the faces of friends, everything."

From similar incidents, Dr. Noyes has concluded that what transpires just before death is like a play in three acts.

Act 1 Dr. Noyes calls "Resistance." The mood is one of panic and desperation played out at a frenzied pace. The actor, alone on the stage, struggles to overcome the forces leading to inevitable death. The climber grabs for a rock or tree branch to break his fall; the exhausted swimmer scans frantically for a floating piece of timber. Hall, in this phase, yanked again and again on the ripcord of his primary chute, then at the auxiliary one, and finally, in sheer panic, he reached around and attempted to tear open his backpack by hand. What is important to realize here is that the real actor in Act 1 is the ego, that ham of wakeful consciousness, determined to hang on, refusing to be upstaged by death. The obsession is to retain the present, the here-and-now in which the self thrives. But in such near-death encounters the ego is fighting a losing battle. And eventually that "actor of actors" sees the fateful odds, makes a compromise, and Act 2 begins.

Dr. Noyes calls this act the "Review of Life." When all chances for survival have been exhausted, the actor submits to a cavalcade of happy memories: family outings, a love affair or two, college days, and the tender times of childhood. All these things and more roll by like an old home movie, all a little yellowed by age and wrapped in the romantic quality of sunlight. For many people the dominant mood of Act 2 is nostalgia. It is interesting to note that if death comes more gradually, as in the case of Dean, the "Review of Life" can often take on a somber, frightening mood in which the person relives experiences that he feels guilty for and wishes to attone. Since the ego can't have the present, it relives the past—anything to escape confrontation with death, an act in which it believes it plays no role.

Dr. Noyes calls Act 3 "Transcendence." When the mind switches off its memory projector, the ego as we normally know it is silenced. It has been written out of the play, and a new character of consciousness enters, a part of ourselves that values the spiritual above the corporeal, a part that we might never have suspected existed within. Since the physical body has become meaningless, smashing into the ground at sixty miles per hour is also meaningless; wakeful life is no longer precious. The spirit has been freed from wakeful constraints and is able to soar above the physical plane—experience an OBE. Bob Hall found it exhilarating. Literary patron Caresse Crosby, who nearly drowned as a child, called it the high point of her life: "I saw the efforts to bring me back to life and I tried not to come back. I was only seven, a carefree child, but that moment in all my life has never been equaled for pure happiness." Albert Heim, a Swiss geologist who fell while climbing the Alps in 1892, was prompted by his own transcendent experience to collect information from thirty others who, like himself, had survived mountain falls. Heim found that just seconds before their "death," they felt detached from their body, heard heavenly music, saw magnificent lights, and were washed in feelings of peace and reconciliation. The people did not regret "dying"; in fact, they said that if given the choice, they would not have returned to life.

It is interesting to note the differences between the experiences resulting from sudden death as studied by Dr. Noyes and Albert Heim, and those told by some people revived from clinical death. The approach of sudden death plays itself out in three distinct acts. On the other hand, people who experience clinical death on the operating table—while they are already unconscious due to shock or anesthesia—witness only Act 3. They are spared the always unpleasant Act 1 and the occasionally unpleasant Act 2. Like late theater-goers, they arrive at their seats just in time for the show's climax. It is quite possible that failed suicides who get as far as having a transcendent experience might be tempted to go back and try again—perhaps with more success on the next location.

Dean, the twenty-six-year-old black man, experienced Death Encounters of the First and Second Kind. He had a subjective, very beautiful experience and he also provided factual evidence that he had been aware of his surroundings while he was unconscious. Drs. Grof and Halifax have also seen Death Encounters of the Third and Fourth Kinds.

Matthew was a forty-two-year-old internist suffering from inoperable cancer of the pancreas. When the disease struck him he had a beautiful wife, a good marriage, three children, and a well-established medical practice. The idea of his own death hit him hard, and as his emotional distress grew, he contacted Dr. Grof. (Matthew was well acquainted with his LSD therapy for terminal cancer patients, and he had even referred some of his own patients to Dr. Grof.) On the day of his session, Matthew received 200 micrograms of LSD, and after about an hour he drifted into an altered state of consciousness while listening to classical music that he described as "otherworldly." He uttered fragmented phrases: "One world and one universe . . . all is one . . . nothing and everything . . . the glittering extremities of his majesty's possession . . . so I am immortal . . . it is true!" Deborah, his wife, could not believe such statements were coming from her pragmatic, analytical husband.

Matthew expressed his LSD experience as "being in a warm cocoon, surrounded by unending love, feeling helpless, but happy and safe." His most powerful experience was lying on the mattress with Deborah, embracing her, and feeling that his body was extending out from its boundaries and melting into hers. After his LSD trip, his view of death changed favorably, but his physical condition worsened. Drs. Grof and Halifax were to go to Hartford, Connecticut, for two days. Worried about leaving Matthew, Dr. Joan Halifax paid him a visit and he calmly told her, "It makes no sense to fight it any longer, if it is time to leave. . . . Do not worry, it is all right." Matthew knew that he was dying. Dr. Halifax wanted desperately to stay with him, but business forced her away.

While she and Dr. Grof were staying at a hotel in Hartford, she woke up at three o'clock in the morning from a dream about Matthew, in which he appeared smiling and repeated the last words he had spoken to her: "It is all right." She had the distinct feeling that Matthew had just died. When they called the hospital the next morning, the attending physician told them that Matthew had died at three o'clock that morning.

Taking mind-altering drugs should not be considered an easy way to glimpse heaven, nor even to get an idea of what it might feel like to die. Psychedelics distort reality, and in some cases they provide the user with a peak experience (good or bad) because they enable him to transcend reality. They may open the doors of perception, but they do not always open the gates of heaven. There is an important difference between a healthy person taking a hallucinogen and the same drug being administered to a terminally ill patient. We have seen evidence that certain physiological and psychological signs of death can start as much as a year before a person dies. The body and the subconscious mind know that death is imminent. In the case of terminally ill patients in the final stages of their disease, there is an additional conscious awareness of death. These factors significantly influence a psychedelic experience by a dying patient to make it different from other drug trips.

Does fear of death motivate our belief in survival? Does our proud ego force upon us the idea of spiritual continuity? After all, a person who knows he is near death has every reason to want to believe in a hereafter.

Any "American Book of the Dead" would have to tackle these issues. Fear of death, we are told, is deeply ingrained. A tremendous amount of research has been done on death and dying, and most of it seems to assume that everybody is naturally afraid to die— that fear of death is programmed into our genes. But a closer look at the vast literature on psychological responses to death suggests that the fear is manifest only in adults and older children, and then only when they have time to dwell on it. There is no evidence that such fear is a natural and inevitable part of our behavior. On the contrary, in cultures where death is dealt with more openly and seen as part of the living process, there is no fear of dying. "In other species," observed biologist Lyall Watson, "there is nothing to show that death is one of the stimuli that release instinctive avoidance or distress responses. When young chimpanzees reach a certain age, they will, without instruction or training, avoid contact with snake-like objects. They have built-in tendency to react fearfully to stimuli that could be associated with danger, but I do not know of a single organism that manifests a natural fear of death itself." Thus, we are taught to fear death, and there is every indication that with the proper training and preparation we can completely overcome that fear. To see how this can be done—to learn the "art of dying"—we have only to look to the East.

Tibetan monks have been telling people how to die for centuries. We do not mean counseling the terminally ill and their families to help them accept disease and its inevitable consequences. This is another, and very much needed, service, one that is slowly growing in this country. By the "art of dying" we are referring to the more paranormal aspects of death.

Reports from the brink of death tell us that dying can be far less fearsome than commonly thought, and that the moment of death need not be an emotional catastrophe but, properly prepared, it can be a delight. In fact, if from an early age we were schooled in the art of dying as taught by Eastern sects, it would not be necessary to counsel terminally ill patients or their families. Twenty-six-year-old Loretta Sykes learned this the hard way.

Loretta discovered that the extreme lethargy she had

been feeling for over a year was due to leukemia. As her condition worsened, she had to quit her job as a waitress in Boston and spend a good deal of her time resting at home. Soon she learned that radiation treatments were not arresting the disease and that she might have to be hospitalized. Though her doctors could not tell her how long she might live, she felt that her time was brief. A few months at most. Emotionally, she found the prospect of dying impossible to accept. She had been raised a Roman Catholic but had "abandoned the faith" in college when she found that "it was not intellectually satisfying." On the verge of death, formal religion seemed no more appealing. "My doctors were really kind," she said, "but they were no real help. Two friends did me the most good." Her friends, a married couple her own age, had heard that a Tibetan Buddhist monastery had recently opened in New York's Duchess County, headed by the fifteenth Gyalwa Karmapa. The lama, who had come from India to found the monastery, was an authority on instructing the dying. Too feeble to travel to New York, through the help of her friends Loretta eventually located an Indian-born pandit who had been trained in the Tibetan way of death.

Two evenings a week he read to her from the *Tibetan Book of the Dead* and from his own writings on death, explaining the basic Eastern philosophy. It helped greatly. Loretta learned that death is but one moment in a continuous flow of experiences that extends from before birth to beyond death; that birth and death recur continually throughout one's lifetime; that if a person can maintain a clear and steady state of mind while dying, the experience of death can be spiritual and liberating; and that the mourning of friends and loved ones can make dying more difficult, prolonging the departure of the soul and thwarting spiritual liberation.

She learned too that there are distinct events that occured after death, called "bardos." A succession of bardo experiences begins as one dies and continues for the next forty-nine days. The bardos are composed of heavens and hells, demons and Buddhas. Her instructor told her that each of these symbols represents a state of mind. The bardos re-create the major mental states, habits, and memories of the dying person's life. The realm of hell, for example, is a crescendo of confusing emotions that generate paranoid terror.

Each bardo can be either a trap or a door to freedom, depending on how one approaches it. The bardo of the jealous gods, for example, arises as the result of the envy the dying person felt during his life. To be either afraid of or attracted to these awesome apparitions dooms one to their particular hell; but to view them calmly, merely as projections of one's mind, makes dying easy.

Loretta's instructor told her that she might glimpse all sorts of traumatic visions but that if she relaxed and flowed with whatever was happening to her, she would experience only peace and calmness; only when a person resists does the hallucination manifest itself emotionally. It was advice that young Loretta could relate to. She occasionally smoked marijuana, and in college she had tried several types of hallucinogens. She knew that to resist a hallucination could be pleasant. Loretta found it easy to believe that frightening death hallucinations are only negative projections of the mind. In the Tibetan teachings she saw a comforting roadmap through death, and she had a personal bridge that linked the Tibetan way to something she had previously experienced. When we last spoke with Loretta she was still undergoing medical treatments, and although her prognosis was no better, her mental state had greatly improved. She said that she still does not want to die, but if death is inevitable, she is prepared to go through it fearlessly.

For many, one of the most appealing aspects of the Tibetan teachings is the view that death is nothing more than a shift in consciousness, a transfer of the mind to a higher plane, and that every time a Buddhist meditates he experiences a form of death. Final death just takes place without the physical body.

This teaching is at the core of the philosophy taught at the Buddhist community Vajradhatu in Boulder, Colorado. It was started by the lama Chogyam Trungpa and is run today by his American-born disciple Osel Tendzin. With about six hundred followers, the community teaches people of all ages how to die and works closely with the terminally ill. Other communities have sprung up. The Institute for the Development of the Harmonious Human Being, in Crestline, California, run by Eastern-trained E. J. Gold, specializes in the "teaching of conscious death." Dr. John Lilly, a leading scientist in mind research, believes that Gold's philosophy— an amalgam of Eastern and Western concepts—is a major breakthrough in understanding death and rebirth.

The crux of dying, Gold teaches, is being able to maintain awareness through the entire "death-transit-rebirth" process. (By "rebirth" Gold refers to the reemergence of consciousness on a higher plane of existence, not necessarily bodily reincarnation—a process that can come much later.) In order to avoid going unconscious or "blank" at the time of death, and thus missing the death experience, one must be prepared. The specific training needed to die consciously is not simply a matter of becoming intellectually familiar with a description of the death experience, said Gold. "Since the intellect itself is going to dissolve during transit, a deeper level of preparation is necessary if one is not to be overwhelmed and driven into unconscious rebirth." Gold believes that this lack of preparation for death and conscious rebirth might explain why only about fifteen percent of the people resuscitated from clinical death have experiences to report. It is something in these people's makeup that permits them to "remain awake" during their death, while others are revived and remember nothing.

For the last ten years Gold has trained hundreds of people in the "science of conscious death." The prophet Muhammed's advice, "Die before you die," is Gold's motto, for he believes that a person must experience death (or a mini-death) in this life if he is to have control over the events of his final departure from the physical world. The death that Gold advocates, via certain meditation exercises and self-induced, self-controlled OBEs, is the "release from the tendency to cling to illusion"—the illusion of death as an end, and the falsehood of this physical life being the only life. "This is the only real death," said Gold. "Once you learn that *life* is the transitory illusion—however real it appears during its duration—then you've mastered dying."

Gold's maxim, "Life is the illusion," has attracted many followers, but his techniques are long and require great concentration and devotion. They also require a willingness to abandon many cherished Western notions. A more Western preparation for death, and a far more practical one in the eyes of the medical profession, is offered by Dr. J. William Worden, professor of psychology at Harvard University and director of Project Omega—a notable eight-year study of terminal illness and death, conducted at Massachusetts General Hospital in Boston.

Dr. Worden has developed a fascinating program called Personal Death Awareness (PDA) and has written lucidly about it in his book of the same name. Anyone can take Dr. Worden's "test" to measure his PDA, and the results can be amazing. Terminally ill patients claim that it has changed their last few weeks of life, and even healthy people who have taken the test come away with an entirely new perspective on death. Dr. Worden's program measures how ready you are for your own death, how that readiness (or lack of it) influences your everyday life, and how by raising your PDA quotion you not only lose your fear of death but view life in richer, nobler, and more realistic terms. The PDA test emerged from years of observation of dying patients and their families. Here is a very small sample of the kinds of questions that patients (or healthy people) are required to answer in depth:

At what age do you expect to die?

When would you like to die? Why?

How would you best like to die? Choose and explain the way.

How would you least like to die? Why?

Write your own obituary.

How will people remember you?

How do you want to be remembered?

Draw a picture of how you view death.

If you were terminally ill, would you want to know you were dying?

What would you give up now to extend your life? One arm? A leg? An eye?

Draw up a will now.

Who would you like to be present when you die? Why?

When I think of death I think of . . . (Complete the sentence.)

The questions run on and on. There are multiple choice: How do you feel about death at this moment? You are given a selection of twenty adjectives to choose from: frightened, indifferent, happy, etc. Through all this, Dr. Worden scores you, and he has defined personality types based on PDA results. "I have given the test to colleagues," he told us, "and found that it changes their perspective on death."

The premise underlying Dr. Worden's test is simple enough. A major obstacle to getting on proper terms with life is the inability of most people to come to grips with the inevitability of death. "Intellectually," said Dr.

Worden, "we know our bodies will perish and rot, but emotionally we are so scared of dying that we disguise it as 'passing on,' or the 'big sleep.' " Do we not paint and dress corpses to look shockingly alive?

For the elderly, sickly, or terminally ill, taking Dr. Worden's test can be particularly enlightening. It makes them confront a close-at-hand reality (one that exists at a subconscious level in everyone's mind). And by raising that issue to full conscious awareness, profound personality changes occur. For one, the will to live can be so strongly rekindled that a patient simply refuses to die when his time has come. And succeeds.

One of the most remarkable cases of a person living far beyond medical predictions was related by Bob Reeves, a chaplain at Columbia Presbyterian Hospital in New York City. A friend of his, dying of cancer, told him that it was very important for her to live to see the New Year, which was still several months away. She even bet the chaplain a dollar that she would live until the New Year. Happy that she was able to face the subject of her own death so naturally, he accepted her challenge, but neither of them informed her family of the wager. On New Year's Eve, Chaplain Reeves spent the evening with the woman and her relatives. At the stroke of midnight, everyone sang and raised glasses in a toast to the New Year, and the sick woman, sitting in the family circle in her wheelchair, extended her open palm to Reeves and smiled as he reached into his pocket and handed her a dollar bill. She accepted it, grasped it tightly, folded her hands in her lap, and died. She had kept herself alive through the strength and force of her spirit, and lengthened her life until she reached the deadline she had set for herself.

Sometimes the will to live can be wrapped up in the sick person's sense of responsibility toward his family. One autumn Dr. Worden saw a young mother who had a terminal case of cancer. After she learned that her condition was rapidly getting worse and that she might not live past the end of the year, Dr. Worden could almost see the will power surge up in her face. Thinking of her small children, she declared, "I'll be damned if I'll die at Christmas and always have my kids associate that happy holiday with my death." The woman struggled past Christmas season with tremendous determination and fortitude. January had almost come to a close when she finally died.

The foregoing cases point to the fact that *death is often a state of mind,* and that the death instinct, and the ability to turn it on and off, is rooted deep in our subconscious.

7

Death, When Is Thy Sting?

"Death will come when thou art dead," wrote the poet Shelley in *To Night*. Ah! if only the moment of death were that easy to peg down.

Joseph B. Kennedy thought he saw his thirteen-year-old daughter, Jolene, die the night of July 15, 1974, in a hospital room in High Point, North Carolina. Bedside, he listened as her breathing slowed and then stopped. He held her frail hand and felt it gradually grow cold as her pulse weakened. Finally, he watched her pupils dilate and her eyes fix in the "death stare" that he remembered from distant days as a Methodist chaplain ministering to the dying at an Atlanta hospital. After Jolene was pronounced dead, Joseph Kennedy gave permission for her useful organs to be removed and frozen for transplant purposes; then he left the hospital and began making funeral arrangements so that the body of his daughter could be cremated.

In the operating room of the High Point Memorial Hospital, Dr. Charles Rowe was preparing to remove Jolene's eyes and kidneys. He had scrubbed in, all the surgical equipment was laid neatly on a green cloth near his elbow, and he was just about to make an incision in Jolene's right eye to remove the cornea, when suddenly she began to breathe again—faintly, but under her own power.

Joseph Kennedy was accepting condolences from relatives when he received the news that Jolene was alive. "I wanted to beat someone up," he recalled. "I wanted to kiss the doctor. I was hit with so many emotions I cannot describe them all. I wanted to run up and down the hospital halls." Had the doctor who pronounced Jolene dead blundered? Not likely. It's just that the moment of death is becoming more and more difficult to determine.

With that difficulty comes some very scary possibilities: Are people's organs ever removed before they are *really* dead? Is it possible that a person out of his body watches doctors abandon resuscitation efforts and sees his body pronounced dead, covered with a sheet, and wheeled into a storage freezer? Might he be begging them all the while to try again, harder, to revive him? Doctors themselves are worried about these possibilities.

Confusion in determining the real moment of death also creates legal problems. Hugh Smith and his wife, Lucy, were in a car accident. Hugh was found dead at the scene of the crash; his wife, unconscious, was taken to a hospital. The couple had no children and in each of their wills they had named the other as executor. On probate of the estate, a lawyer noted that Mrs. Smith was the survivor even though she never regained consciousness and died in the hospital seventeen days after the accident. Thus, Mrs. Smith inherited her husband's entire estate, which then passed on to her descendants. Hugh Smith's relatives disagreed with that decision. A nephew petitioned the court and argued that both Hugh and Lucy Smith, "deceased, lost their power to will at the same instant and that their demise as earthly human beings occurred at the same time in the automobile accident." The court, leaning on a 1951 legal definition of death, ruled that "a person breathing, though unconscious, is not dead." The estate went to Lucy Smith's heirs.

Not many years ago it was easy to tell if a person was dead. You held a cold, dry mirror in front of the person's face, or spit tobacco juice into the person's eye and checked for a reflex. Or you could feel for a pulse and listen for heartbeats. These were all considered reliable methods, for death meant simply the cessation of heart and lung activity. Lucy Smith's case extended the definition of death in the state of North Carolina to include brainwave activity. The subtleties are growing finer and finer each day. The very technology that is used to prolong life has made it almost impossible to determine the moment of death. Artificial respirators and heart-and-lung machines keep the body alive, and the electroencephalograph has shown that a person can produce strong brainwaves even after his heart and lungs have stopped functioning. In fact, many doctors now believe that what has always been called the "moment of death" may not even exist.

"There is no magical moment when life disappears," said Robert S. Morison, professor of science at Cornell University. "Death is no more a single, clearly delimited, momentary phenomenon than is infancy, adolescence, or middle age." The gradualness of dying is clearer today than ever, said Morison. "We know that various parts of the body can go on living for months after its central organization has disintegrated." That fact not only has medical and legal ramifications, but religious ones as well. If death is a gradual process, when does the soul, or what French philosopher Henri Bergson called *l'elan vital,* which separates man from other living creatures on earth, depart the body? Theologians may take their time grappling over that question, but doctors and lawyers require an immediate answer.

Michael Schwed knows this. In July 1977 his five-year-old daughter, Laura, complained of a severe sore throat. She was found to be suffering from a bacterial infection known as Hemophilus influenza type B, which attacks the epiglottis and obstructs breathing. The infection spread so quickly that before the Schweds could get their daughter to the Nassau County Medical Center on Long Island, her breathing had been impaired for an hour. Laura was near death on arrival and was placed on a respirator. Her doctors were certain that she had suffered massive brain damage. After a week had passed, an EEG was performed to measure the extent of the damage. It showed no brain activity whatsoever. Laura Schwed was dead. Or was she?

In New York State, the legislature has never legalized the definition of "brain death," even though hospitals use it daily. Michael Schwed argued that as long as his daughter's body was alive he wanted every effort made to revive her, and he brought legal action against the hospital when they lowered Laura's level of care. At this time the case is still pending. Michael Schwed feels that his daughter still possesses the "vital glow." "In my mind," he said, "a miracle is still possible. I'm going to do everything possible to give Laura a chance to come back." The success doctors have had in reviving people from clinical death has given many families hope—sometimes justified, sometimes not.

In 1968 a group of Harvard physicians defined "brain death." Under the widely accepted definition, a person must display a flat EEG for twenty-four hours; then, after a lapse of time, he must be checked again, and if the EEG is still flat, the person is dead. This assumes that the person has suffered an irreversible coma and that if he were ever resuscitated from this state he would live a vegetative existence.

Many states besides New York have never legalized the definition of "brain death." Now, a new auditory device, developed by Dr. Arnold Starr, a neurologist at the University of California, Irvine, may complicate the brain-death definition—and for some cases, make it obsolete. Starr's device, which is one thousand times more sensitive than the EEG, monitors electrical activity deep in the center of the brain. Already Dr. Starr has shown that twenty-six people who were pronounced dead by the conventional flat EEG standards were in fact alive, and some of these people were revived— without brain damage!

The issue of brain death may become even more clouded. In a dramatic experiment, an Ontario neurologist recently demonstrated that EEG readings cannot always be trusted. Dr. Adrian Upton of McMaster University in Hamilton, Ontario, made a brainwave analysis of a brain-size mold of lime Jell-o. To many physicians' dismay, he obtained readings that could easily be interpreted as evidence of life. The experiment was conducted in the intensive care unit of a hospital, and the squiggly lines from the Jell-o reflected stray electrical signals given off by nearby respirators, intravenous feeders, and human activity. The experiment was something of a joke, but Dr. Upton was making a serious point in the debate over how to determine the moment of death. "It is extremely difficult to get a flat EEG even in the presence of brain death," said Dr. Upton. "There are hundreds of artifacts that can produce spurious readings."

Dr. Henry Beacher, the distinguished physician who headed the 1968 Harvard Committee that proposed the irreversible-coma definition of death, stated when he announced the Harvard criteria "that whatever level [of brainwave activity] we choose, it is an arbitrary decision," implying that as electronic equipment becomes more sophisticated, what was once detected as a flat EEG will be picked up as ripples characteristic of life. Dr. Arnold Starr's auditory device has already confirmed Dr. Beecher's prediction. When, the concerned person asks, is a person dead beyond the point where he can be returned to life?

Many physicians are not comfortable with the idea of brain death. After a patient has displayed a flat EEG for twenty-four hours, many doctors do not automatically pronounce the patient dead. Instead, they turn off the respirator for about five minutes before pronouncing the patient dead; then they start the respirator again in order to preserve the patient's organs. This practice has led lawyers to ask: why did the doctor turn off the respirator to make the pronouncement of death? Wasn't the flat EEG satisfactory? As one lawyer who observed a doctor's procedure at bedside put it: "Did the doctor do this to satisfy himself and others that the patient had died 'all the way'? If so, it implies to me that the patient might be considered still living at least 'part of the way.'" Michael Schwed was equally suspicious of his daughter's brain death. "The EEG came out flat," he said, "but machines can be wrong. They only did it one time. I'm not satisfied Laura is dead."

False hope can be a crueler burden to bear than the pain of the quick death of a loved one. Clearly, guidelines are needed—ones agreed upon by lawyers, doctors, and theologians. But such harmony is far off, for the problems surrounding death get even more difficult when we consider the "process" of dying.

Is death a process or an event? This is not just an exercise in semantics. It makes a real difference. We think of death as a clearly defined event, an abrupt step that puts a sharp end to life. On the other hand, "dying" is seen as a long drawn-out process that begins when life itself begins and is not completed until the last cell of the body expires.

The first view is the more traditional one, and it is deeply embedded in our literature, art, and law. The "moment of death" notion is probably rooted in the observation of a dramatic, single violent act like the last gasp for breath. "Observers of such a climactic

116

agony have found it easy to believe that a special event of major consequence has taken place," said Dr. Morison, "that death has come and life has gone away." That view is also welcomed by some physicians and theologians because it frees them from facing certain unsettling facts. Today, many scientists are arguing that this Western view of death as an abrupt transition is largely responsible for our ignorance and fear of dying.

An unprejudiced look at the biological facts reveals that our notion of death is as ambiguous as our notion of birth. The living human being starts inconspicuously, unconsciously, and at an unknown time, with the conjugation of two haploid cells. In a matter of hours, this new cell begins to divide. The number of living cells in the organism continues to increase for about the next twenty-five years, then begins slowly to decrease. (This is the biological dividing line between "young" and "old.") Looked at this way, we spend most of our life dying.

"For various reasons," said Dr. Morison, "it is easier to recognize the process at the beginning, birth, than at the end, death." The growing fetus is said to become steadily more "valuable" with the passage of time; its organization becomes increasingly complex and its potential for a healthy, productive life increases. At the other end of life the process is reversed; it is said that the life of the dying patient becomes steadily less complicated and rich, and, as a result, less worth living or preserving. Thus, what was once valuable is now valueless. Right or wrong, that is how the traditional argument goes.

According to a standard medical text, *clinical death* occurs when spontaneous respiration and heartbeat irreversibly cease. The blood stops circulating and the brain is deprived of oxygen. Unless artificial resuscitation is started soon, *brain death* follows: the brain, at normal body temperature, cannot survive without oxygen for more than five minutes. Employing this fact, Assistant District Attorney Thomas J. Mundy argued a landmark brain-death case in the summer of 1976 before the Massachusetts Supreme Court.

At 2:10 P.M. on August 24, 1975, Ronald Salem, thirty-four, a Caucasian, stopped to purchase cigarettes at a corner store in Columbia Point, a predominately black housing project in Boston's Dorchester section. As he returned to his car he was slammed on the head with a baseball bat by eighteen-year-old Seigfried Golston. Surgeons at Boston City Hospital operated in vain; two later tests for brainwaves showed none. Ronald Salem was dead. Doctors removed Salem from the life-support systems and Golston was charged with first-degree murder. The defense attorney argued that the doctors, not Golston, technically killed Salem, and that if the doctors had made a more valiant effort Salem might have lived. Anyway, the attorney argued, his client was guilty only of beating the deceased, not of killing him. Finally, in the spring of 1977 the Massachusetts court disagreed, and in doing so it became the first of the nation's highest state courts to accept the brain-death standard. "Medically speaking," prosecutor Mundy told the court, "even though the heart and circulation have stopped, a person is not actually dead until the brain cells die."

All ten million brain cells? Half of them? Mundy, of course, never specified how many. Nor did he ever consider the question. But doctors who are trying to define death must face the tricky issue.

Just as the body dies in steps, so too does the brain. In oxygen starvation, called anoxia, the first part of the brain to die is the highly evolved cerebral cortex, the section of the brain where sensations are registered and voluntary actions are initiated. The cerebral cortex is the part of the brain that participates in memory storage, where decisions are made and higher thought processes such as language, logic, and mathematics occur.

The midbrain is next to die, then finally the brain stem. If there is irreversible destruction of the higher levels of the brain, the cerebrum, without damage to the brain stem—the primitive, vital center in the lower levels of the nervous system—there is permanent loss of consciousness, but heart and breathing functions can go on. Apparently, more of Salem's brain was damaged since his breathing had to be mechanically supported. When all the components of the brain are dead, *biological death,* or the permanent extinction of bodily life, occurs. Yet, even after biological death, organs within the lifeless body can be kept alive for a time by mechanical or chemical means. In fact, if a guillotine has cut off a man's head, it is possible today to keep his heart and lungs and limbs alive for several days.

Many body cells, however, continue to live on their own for some time after biological death. Muscles, for example, will respond to electrical stimuli for up to two hours. Hair and nails may continue to grow for twenty-four hours or longer. There are many documented cases of exhumed bodies displaying long fingernails and hair. On the other hand, groups of cells can even be removed from the body after death and kept alive and functioning, sometimes indefinitely, in an artificial tissue culture.

At the core of the life-death issue is the difficult distinction between living and nonliving matter. If you define life as the ability to replicate and group—a common definition in biology—the term has fuzzy boundaries. Worker bees, for example, are sterile and therefore cannot copy themselves. Certainly this does not mean that they are dead. Viruses are particularly paradoxical, displaying the reproductive and colonizing traits of living organisms and the structure of inanimate crystals. There is much interest today in whether space probes will find life on the other planets of our solar system. A third possibility, seldom considered, is that the probes may find something that no one will know whether to call living or not.

On November 3, 1977, scientists at the University of Illinois announced that they had found a rare group of bacteria that thrive on hydrogen, carbon dioxide, and heat, and abhor oxygen—in fact, oxygen kills them. The organisms, which are believed to be the oldest yet known—four billion years old—are genetically so different from anything known to exist that Dr. Carl Woese, leader of the research team, has described them as a brand-new "third kingdom" of living material. The bacteria, found in such oxygen-free places as the digestive systems of grazing animals, rotting sewage, and geothermal hot springs, also contain vitamins found nowhere else on earth. Since the early atmosphere of the earth consisted largely of hydrogen and carbon dioxide and was much hotter than it is today, Dr. Woese speculates that the newly found form of life might have been responsible for "eating up" the noxious atmosphere and thereby producing the oxygen environment in which animal life developed; the original bacteria would have been forced into oxygen-free seclusion. Considering the bizarre chemistry of various planets, it is difficult to speculate what forms of life will be found and whether, by earth standards, they will be classified as living or nonliving matter. The spectrum of life may be far broader than we suspect, fading back to the nonliving world of crystals, fading forward to one-cell organisms, and blossoming in hostile atmospheres on nearby planets.

HeLa cells, for instance, present a case that lends itself to profound biological and philosophical speculation. The cells belong to a woman who died in Baltimore more than a quarter of a century ago—a woman who may be as close to actual immortality as anybody on this planet is likely to come. Although she is long dead and buried, cells from her cervix live on in laboratories around the world. "HeLa" is a contraction for her name, which still appears frequently in scientific journals, and her enzymatic and chromosomal signatures are still the standards by which other cell behaviors are measured. The story of Mrs. He—— La—— is worth pursuing.

In February 1951 a young black woman came to the gynecology clinic at Baltimore's Johns Hopkins Hospital. She was suffering from frequent and irregular vaginal bleeding. Upon examination, her doctors found a soft, bleeding area on the cervix, which turned out to be cancerous. At this time scientists had not been successful in incubating and cultivating cancer cells for study. For some unknown reason, a few cells of this woman's cancer responded propitiously to culture techniques, and soon doctors at Johns Hopkins were sending out large quantities of hospital-grown cancer cells, which quickly became the worldwide standard in cancer research. Every laboratory has worked with them. In fact, cancer research today would be years behind if it had not been for the HeLa cells. To this day, each cell contains all the genetic information of the Baltimore woman whom doctors had for years called Helen Lane. However, in 1971 her real identity became known—she was Henrietta Lacks—and journalists beseiged the Lacks family with thoughtless questions as to how they felt about their mother still living in the form of cell cultures. At first the family was shocked at the revelation—they had never even heard of HeLa cells—but gradually they came to view the phenomenon as their mother's contribution to science. Some people donate their organs at death; Henrietta Lacks unknowingly donated her renegade cells. Cloning—that is, making an entire organism from the genetic information in one cell—is not yet possible with humans, but it has been done with certain lower forms of life. If human cloning ever becomes a reality —and many scientists believe it is only a matter of time—can Henrietta Lacks "come back"? If so, will she have a soul? Will any person cloned from the genetic information in a single cell have a soul? This could give theologians the greatest challenge in the history of religion.

Equally valid, and more immediately relevant, is the question: Is there *human* life in the muscles that still reflex two hours after death? In the hair and nails that continue to grow in the grave? Of course, most of us answer, No! Because we mean something very specific when we use the word *life*—we mean the personality of the person. Pope Pius XII, when asked when death occurs, answered: "Human life continues for as long as its vital functions, distinguished from the simple biological life of the organs, manifest themselves spontaneously without the help of artificial processes." But what is the "life force" that makes some cells grow after death? And how is that force related to the life force that characterized the whole living person? Although we talk about "biological forces" and "spiritual forces" and distinguish between physical electromagnetic auras and spiritual auras such as the soul, we have to admit that at present we are still far from possessing the ultimate answers. As straightforward as Pope Pius's definition seems, many physical scientists, and more psychical researchers, argue that it has several serious loopholes. For instance: At exactly what point in the dying process does the personality *permanently* leave the body, never to return? As thousands of resuscitation cases suggest, the personality, or consciousness, can arbitrarily hover, linger, retreat, or return.

A nurse at New York's Flower Fifth Avenue Hospital told a disturbing story of a thirteen-year-old girl whose mother had been resuscitated from clinical death during an emergency hysterectomy. Later, at home, Mrs. Sharon DeMarco shared her OBE experience with her husband, two sons, and daughter. She had drifted above the operating table, and, while watching the resuscitation procedures, part of her consciousness had also traveled across town to her daughter's high school, where she observed a class in progress. Maintaining almost a double awareness at times, Sharon DeMarco later told her doctor fragments of the conversation that had taken place in the operating room. "He turned white," she says now, "and he would not confirm or deny what I knew I heard." Her doctor still refuses to discuss the case, but Mrs. De-Marco's daughter, Donna, was impressed with her mother's observations of the classroom. All Sharon DeMarco had seen was her daughter sitting in the back of a room (her regular seat is nearer the center of the room); she could not identify the class in session, any other people, or events—nothing that could be verified. Donna, however, did not need verification; her mind was working on another track.

Later that night, when her mother came to her room to say good-night, Donna said, "I'm afraid of being buried alive." At first her mother made little of what seemed to be a sudden random fear, but as she sat on her daughter's bed, the full meaning of the statement dawned on her. "Whatever made you think of that?" she asked, suspecting that she already knew the answer. Her daughter answered with a perplexing question: "If you can still be conscious when they say you're dead, couldn't they bury you while you watch everything?" Suddenly Sharon DeMarco envisioned her consciousness lingering on through her funeral services and burial. She answered, "No, absolutely not. That's preposterous," but the question kept her awake that night. The more she ruminated, the more plausible her daughter's speculation seemed. Had she been dead or hadn't she? What would have happened if the doctors had given up on her? Would she have continued to be aware of the events in the operating room?

One chilling question seemed to generate another. She knew that for successful transplants, certain organs must be taken within an hour after death; otherwise, irreversible deterioration sets in. She wondered if it was possible for doctors to give up resuscitation efforts, pronounce a patient dead, and begin removing vital organs, while the patient painlessly observed these procedures from above the operating table. "I was completely aware of everything they were doing to my body," she said. Sharon DeMarco's abdomen was already cut open and doctors were removing some female organs while she "watched." If they had given up trying to revive her when her heart stopped and decided to remove her kidneys for transplant purposes, would she not have observed that too?

In the past, people were sometimes mistakenly pronounced dead and buried alive. Today, since bodies are embalmed, the chance of being buried alive is virtually nonexistent. Yet, Sharon DeMarco's questions have never been answered to her complete satisfaction. Many doctors we spoke with seemed perplexed by the question: When does consciousness begin and end?

The case of Sharon DeMarco happened in 1973, four years before the bestselling novel *Coma* was made into a movie. The story, by Boston eye surgeon Dr. Robert Cook, follows the adventures of a young female doctor who attempts to uncover the reason for a rash of suspicious deaths in a Boston hospital. She discovers that a group of doctors, involved in blackmarketing human organs, has been killing off patients to get their vitals. Dr. Cook's story is so compelling because it is based on suspicions that have concerned doctors and lawyers since the first organ transplants began almost two decades ago. Today, organs are in critically short supply; the lives of many thousands of people hinge on the quick deaths of donors.

A glance at statistics reveals the scope of the problem—and perhaps the seriousness of the consequences. The seven major organ shortages in the United States as of 1977 were:

Kidneys. At the end of 1975 more than fourteen thousand people in the United States had received kidney transplants. About eight thousand people die each year because there are not enough kidneys to go around. Kidneys must be removed within an hour after death.

Eyes. About four thousand cornea transplants are done annually. Doctors estimate that approximately thirty thousand men and women who are partially or totally blind could regain most of their sight if more corneas were available. Eyes are removed from donors about six hours after death.

Ears. Only the inner ear mechanism is used. The Temporal Bond Bank in Maryland does not have figures on how many deaf people could have their hearing restored if more of the needed organs were available. They admit that the figure is in the thousands and that there is a great shortage in this area.

Hearts. Despite all the attention that this type of transplant received starting in the late 1960s, because of the difficulty of the operation and the rate of failure, to date only about 250 heart transplants have been done. However, there is a tremendous shortage of hearts for research cardiology. No numbers are possible, since every heart could conceivably be put to some research use.

Skin and Bones. Skin and bone tissue are collected immediately after death by the United states Naval Tissue Bank in Bethesda, Maryland. Skin is badly needed as a dressing in cases of severe and extensive burns; it is more effective than ordinary cloth bandages. Since large quantities of skin are often needed, the shortage here is great.

Pituitary Glands. This pea-size organ is located beneath the brain. Currently about five thousand children suffer from hypotuitarism, a deficiency in their growth glands that causes them to remain dwarfes. Each of these children needs the extracts from 120 adult glands every year until he reaches full adult size. In other words, to meet the need completely, about seventy-five percent of all those who die in this country each year—or over a million people—would have to donate their glands to the National Pituitary Agency if these children are to grow to normal size.

Given the great shortages in vital organs, recently there has been much speculation that doctors may not always wait long enough before removing organs for transplants. In one widely publicized case, Dr. Norman Shymway, the noted Stanford University heart surgeon, removed the heart from a murder victim and implanted it in one of his patients. Although an EEG trace of the victim's brain showed a flat, death response, his heart was still pulsating mildly when Dr. Shymway began to cut it from the patient's chest. The defense for the alleged murderer, attorney Andrew D. Lyons, argued that his client had not killed the patient by shooting him in the head, but that Dr. Shymway had caused the death by removing a still "beating" heart in his eagerness to obtain an organ for one of his patients. The judge eventually rejected the defense's argument, but another California magistrate in a similar case ruled that removal of a beating heart, or one that has been kept alive by mechanical devices, obscures the cause of death.

In an attempt to insure that there is no conflict of interest in the transplant issue—that is, no conflict between your attending physician and the transplant team—there is a general, though unwritten, rule that the two tasks of pronouncing you dead and of removing your organs be kept separate and be decided by each team independently. In other words, the doctor who determines your death cannot be the one who removes your vital organs. Unfortunately, in hospitals where there is a shortage of doctors, or in emergencies where an organ must be removed quickly and only one doctor is available, the rule cannot be observed. In fact, for purposes of convenience to doctors, and for expediency, many hospitals overlook the safety rule. Since it is a fact that conscious awareness can coexist with clinical death, for all we know it might well survive the official pronouncement of brain death and even extend into the realm of biological death and beyond. These possibilities add new and horrific dimensions to the issue of premature organ removal. No patient, of course, could ever awaken from death once his vital organs were removed. But it is not inconceivable that a "dead" patient could awaken to find that his corneas are missing, or that one kidney has been removed and given to someone else. Perhaps in such instances of premature organ removal the astral body wisely refuses to reenter the incomplete physical body, making what could have been a temporary death a permanent one.

While many doctors argue that there are gradual changes in a person at the time of death, there seems to be an equal number of dissenters. Leon Kass, professor of bioethics at the Kennedy Center for Bioethics at Georgetown University, claims that "while dying is often a continuous process, death is not."

What dies, in Kass's view, is the organism as a whole. This, he feels, is not a gradual process but an abrupt event. It is the wholistic view of death. "It is this death," said Kass, "the death of the individual human being, that is important for physicians and for the community, not the death of organs or cells, which are mere parts." Advocates of the wholistic concept of death argue that life, especially human life, cannot be reduced to its physiological, biological, and psychochemical components. In the case of human beings, they claim, the whole is definitely more than the sum of its parts. Further, they contend that all attempts to blur the distinction between life and death are unsound and dangerous. According to this viewpoint, the physical and astral bodies separate abruptly and irreversibly; the silver cord does not slowly stretch and fray but cleanly snaps.

It is apparent that philosophy, ethics, and personal beliefs are as relevant in defining death as are law and medicine. In his book, *Death, Dying and the Biological Revolution,* Robert M. Veatch, who holds a Ph.D. in religion, poses a hypothetical situation that might one day come true, and it touches the core of the life-death argument.

At first, said Veatch, it would appear that the irreversible cessation of heart and lung activity would represent a simple and straightforward statement of the traditional concept of death in Western culture. Yet, upon reflecion even this proves untrue. "If patients simply lose control of their lungs and have to be permanently supported by a mechanical respirator, they are still living persons as long as they continue to get oxygen. If modern technology produces an efficient, compact heart-lung machine capable of being carried on the back or in a pocket, people using such devices would not be considered dead, even though both heart and lungs were permanently nonfunctioning. Some might consider such a technological man an affront to human dignity; some might argue that such a device should never be connected to a human; but even they would, in all likelihood, agree that such people are alive."

A moment's reflection shows that whether one states it or not, the soul is at the heart of the entire life-death debate. If the soul could be identified, located, pinned to one or more physical locations—to the satisfaction of most people—much of the confusion would vanish. In the time of Aristotle, man thought of his soul located in his heart. For Descartes, the soul resided in the pineal gland at the base of the brain. In adopting the modern definition of brain death, are we really saying that man's soul is situated in his brain? It seems we are saying precisely that. Veatch takes this line of reasoning to a chilling extreme. Consider the admittedly remote possibility that the electrical impulses of the brain could be transferred, by recording devices, onto computer tape. Would that tape, together with some kind of minimum sensory device, be a living human being, and would erasure of the tape be considered murder?

This is not so farfetched an idea when we look at the research of Dr. Robert White. At the Cleveland Metropolitan General Hospital, Department of Neurosurgery, Dr. White works in the brain-research laboratory with monkeys. First he anesthetizes a monkey and carefully removes its brain. He discards the body, places the brain in a saline solution, and pumps in oxygen under pressure. Dr. White has kept scores of monkey brains alive for several weeks, and apparently "thinking"; electrodes show that the brains respond normally to electrical stimuli.

Dr. White is attempting to get a better picture of how brains function by studying them in isolation, but his unorthodox research has posed some thorny questions: Is the brain in the jar the whole monkey? If the brainless body of a monkey were kept alive by a heart-and-lung machine (an easy task), would *it* contain the quintessential life of the monkey, or would that reside with the brain in the jar? Where is the monkey's personality? In the body, the jar, or is it somehow divided between the two? Dr. White claims that the isolated brain's activity is actually stronger and clearer than when the brain is attached to the body. Exactly what that means is unclear, but it makes our questions all the more relevant.

One of Dr. White's colleagues, when asked how he knows that the brain in the jar thinks, answered: "We know it through the instruments, the EEG traces. These wires indicate they are connected with a functional brain. No doubt about it. I even suspect that without his [the monkey's] senses, he can think more quickly. What kind of thinking, I don't know. I guess he is primarily a memory, a repository for information stored when he had his flesh; he cannot develop further because he no longer has the nourishment of experience. Yet, this too is a new experiece."

Monkeys were chosen for the research because their brains are so similar to those of humans. Ethics aside for the moment, Dr. White's experiments could just as successfully be carried out with humans. Suddenly our questions urgently demand answers. But they may never really be answered until the experiment is done with a human brain and the brain is successfully implanted back into the skull. Might that person awaken to tell us that he has had a most extraordinary OBE? Is this what the scores of disembodied monkeys experience?

The "nourishment of experience," to use Dr. White's colleague's phrase, is precisely what many scientists and theologians view as a primary requirement for life. It is the higher mental functions of man, said Veatch, "that are so essential that their loss ought to be taken as the death of the person." While consciousness is certainly important, Veatch argues that man's social nature and embodiment seem to be the truly essential characteristics. "I therefore believe that death is most appropriately thought of as the irreversible loss of the embodied capacity for social interaction."

That belief identifies the whole brain as the seat associated with the irreversible loss of bodily integration. The empirical task of determining the criteria for the irreversible loss of bodily integration was carried out in 1968 by Harvard Medical School's Ad Hoc Committee to Examine the Definition of Brain Death.

In addition to a flat EEG for twenty-four hours, the other, deceptively simple, criteria are:

1. The patient should be totally unaware and unresponsive so that "even the most intensely painful stimuli evoke no vocal or other response, not even a groan, withdrawal of a limb, or quickening of respiration."

2. The patient should be observed for at least an hour to make certain that there are no muscular movements or spontaneous breathing.

3. Reflexes should be absent. Tendons tapped with a small reflex hammer should not elicit the reflexive muscular responses seen in a living person. Pupils of the eyes should be dilated and unresponsive to bright light.

All these tests should be repeated at least twenty-four hours later and show no change.

As mentioned earlier, the criteria have become widely recognized, though not so widely adopted legally. Confusion abounds. Since 1970, at least twelve states have enacted legislation on the determination of death, but the criteria differ from state to state—which means death differs from state to state. Kansas, Maryland, New Mexico, Oregon, and Virginia, for example, require the cessation of spontaneous respiratory and cardiac functions or the cessation of spontaneous brain function. Alaska, Michigan, and West Virginia list the cessation of respiratory and circulatory functions and consider irreversible coma a secondary criterion. At the other extreme, Illinois simply makes brain function the measure of life and death. Clearly, there is more confusion than ever as to when a person is both medically and legally dead.

Whether you are alive or dead varies even more depending on the country in which you die. France's National Academy of Medicine considers a person dead if his EEG shows no activity for forty-eight hours. The Soviets use a flat-EEG criterion as short as five minutes in some cases.

Dr. Joseph J. Timmes, professor of surgery at the New Jersey College of Medicine and Dentistry, went to the Soviet Union and spoke to doctors at the medical institutes in Leningrad and Moscow. When asked how they define the moment of death, they answered that this was not a serious problem in the USSR because all bodies belong to the state. "When an individual dies—meaning when he is pronounced dead—physicians can perform an autopsy or remove an organ without consent of the next of kin, as is legally required in the United States," said Dr. Timmes.

And a flat EEG trace can be totally meaningless if a person freezes to death. If a person's body temperature drops below 90° F., the condition called hypothermia sets in. The victim can show a flat EEG for many hours and still be capable of full recovery, without brain damage; in effect, he thaws out. "Under conditions of hypothermia," said one doctor, "although the patient appears dead by all conventional standards, he is actually in a temporary state of artificially induced hibernation or suspended animation." (We will examine some record-breaking cases of hypothermia in the next chapter.)

All of the problems surrounding the determination of death are poignantly illustrated by prize-winning writer B. D. Colen, who investigated the Karen Ann Quinlan case. In his moving book, *Karen Ann Quinlan: Dying in the Age of Eternal Life,* Colen cites the case of a critically injured woman, dead on arrival at a hospital, placed on a respirator and restored to life, until surgeons found that her liver was damaged beyond repair and she could not be saved. They turned off the respirator, allowing her to die a second time. Said Colen: "Some would say that the doctor who turned off the respirator was playing God, that he murdered the woman. If the doctors were playing God, they were doing so when they turned the machines on. For any man can take a life, but those doctors did what we are told only God can do—they gave the woman life." The technology man has developed to prolong life has made dying a complex, ambiguous, and controversial task.

In *King Lear,* Shakespeare described the popular method of his day to see if a person is alive: "Lend me a looking glass; if her breath will mist or stain the stone, why, then she lives." If patients today who were clinically dead were tested with the looking glass, none would be alive. We would have no stories of an afterlife. What will be said in a hundred years of our present-day definitions of death? That we "killed off" more living people than unwitting physicians did in Shakespeare's time?

8

How Death
Affects Life

The late Rabbi Y. M. Tuckachinsky created a parable that neatly summarizes everything we have discussed thus far and anticipates issues that will occupy us throughout the remainder of the book.

Imagine twins growing peacefully in the warmth of the womb. Their lives are serene. Their whole world is the interior of the womb. Who could conceive of anything larger, better, more comfortable?

They feel movement and soon begin to speculate. "We are getting lower and lower. Surely if this continues, we will exit one day. What will happen then?"

Now, one infant is a believer, heir to a religious tradition that tells him there will be a "new life" after this warm and wet existence in the womb. A strange belief, seemingly without foundation, but one to which he holds fast. It is comforting. The second infant is a thoroughgoing skeptic. Mere stories do not deceive him. What is not within one's experience can have no basis in one's imagination.

Says the faithful brother: "After our 'death' here, there will be a new, great word of unfathomable beauty, one richer in experiences. We will eat through the mouth! We will see great distances, and we will hear music and voices through the ears on the sides of our heads."

Replies the skeptic: "Nonsense. You are looking for something to calm your fear of death. There is only this world. There is no world to come! Our world will collapse and we will sink into oblivion. This may not be a comforting thought, but it is a logical one."

Suddenly the water inside the womb bursts. The womb convulses. All hell breaks loose. There is pushing and pulling and pain. A mysterious pounding. Churning. Staccato thrusts. The believing brother throws himself headlong into the experience and flows down a dark tunnel. Tearing himself from the womb, he falls outward, exits. The second brother shrieks and holds back. He is shocked by his mate's accident. He bewails and bemoans the tragedy. Then he hears a bloodcurdling cry, followed by tumultuous shouts from the blackness, then silence. He cries: "Oh my! What a horrible end. Just as I predicted."

"As the skeptic brother mourns, his 'dead' brother has been born into a new world," wrote Rabbi Tuckachinsky. "The cry is a sign of health and vigor, and the tumult is a chorus of joyous sounds by the waiting family for the birth of a healthy child."

Man comes from the darkness of the "not yet" and proceeds to the darkness of the "no more." While we find it difficult to imagine the "not yet," it is even more difficult to imagine the "no more." More than birth, it is the thought of our own death that has the most profound influence on our life. People revived from clinical death find that their experience greatly alters their life. In fact, any brush with death, any kind of death encounter, can have this effect. There is a magic to death.

Scholars agree that if the word death were absent from our vocabulary, our great works of literature would have remained unwritten, pyramids and cathedrals would not exist, nor would works of art—for all art is rooted in religion or magic. The constant reality of death is what gives life its significance and meaning. "Death is the mainspring of our motivations, endeavors, and accomplishments," said one psychologist. According to Freud and Jung, there is not a moment of the day or night, while we are busily active or asleep, when the subconscious is not aware of death. Often that awareness surfaces no matter how hard we might fight it. Alan Watts said, "Nothing is more provocative than the idea of death. It is because men know that they will die that they have created the arts and sciences, the philosophies and religions. For nothing is more thought-provoking than the thought which seems to put an end to thought."

According to psychiatrist Dr. Anthony Storr, man is the only creature who can habitually contemplate his own death. Animals, we know, are endowed with reflexes and automatic responses to danger that protect them against a premature end, but we cannot believe that animals, like man, see death as inescapable at some future date. Our awareness of our own inevitable death may be the single most significant factor separating man from all other living organisms.

All evidence suggests that children become aware of death at around the age of five. This is the time when a child starts to distinguish himself clearly from his environment and other humans; his ego has grown to a stage where he views himself as a separate entity, and once the ego establishes its own supremacy, it immediately begins to contemplate the possibility of its own demise. Depending on how a child is reared, he can conceive of death as a frightening, final, extinguishing experience, or in a more religious view as a sublime continuance of the personality. Either way, death literally haunts him throughout his life.

Prior to age five, children regard talking to deceased relatives (or family members who are not physically present in a room) as common and normal as conversing with a person face to face. Andrew Greeley, director of the National Opinion Research Center of the University of Chicago, surveyed the American public and found that a surprising thirty-one percent of the teen-agers questioned felt that they had been in contact with the dead at least once. "The high score among teen-agers," said Greeley, "is hard to explain." Unfortunately, no one has conducted a study on contact with the dead by very young children. There is a wealth of anecdotal evidence, but a rigorous study might show that many children are not fantasizing when they claim to have talked with deceased relatives. Being unaware of the so-called boundary between life and death, they might cross it easily. Children assume a perfect continuity between all things, not at all unlike the "interconnectedness" of nature observed by modern physicians. Studies of children from China, Hungary, Sweden, Switzerland, and the United States all show that before age six, children view life as everlasting. Psychiatrists make light of this. Are we to assume that this is merely a silly, "childish" notion, or is there a very profound truth to be learned from such evidence?

One five-year-old girl revived from drowning reported her OBE to her doctor and her parents as though it were as natural as taking a walk. She saw nothing incongruous in the fact that her body could be on the beach, surrounded by people, while she was floating in the air: she was not dead, she said, just going on an adventure. Might a child's remarks reflect some innate human potential for OBEs and a fundamental knowledge of survival?

Psychologist M. Eissler gives three reasons why scientists have for decades avoided death as a field of study: (1) Pragmatism: since death is universal and inevitable, what can we possibly benefit from a study of it; it's a situation we have no control over; (2) Objectivity: we are too emotionally involved with the topic of death to adopt the required objectivity characteristic of any scientific research; (3) Hedonism: in our culture, energy is invested for the sake of increasing comfort and pleasure; how could a study of such a morbid topic as death contribute to this goal? So far, we have seen that categories 1 and 3 are no longer valid—what we have learned about death in just the last few years from people who have come back constitutes the best evidence yet for survival.

Other studies of death are shedding more light on life. Dr. Lisl Marburg Goodman, a psychologist at Jersey City State College in New Jersey, conducted 623 in-depth interviews with creative people and concluded that creativity and the fear of death are linked in ways more intricate than scientists previously thought. Most highly creative people were willing to talk freely about their own eventual death and said that they felt no particular anxiety about it. But on probing further, Dr. Goodman found many contradictions. The case of a young physicist is a perfect example.

Highly regarded in his field, an innovative thinker, K.M. claimed that he had long ago accepted the idea of death as inevitable and therefore "never gave it a second thought." No, he said, the idea of dying did not depress him, nor did talk about death; and certainly thoughts of death did not motivate his activites or inspire him even in subliminal ways. At this point in the interview Dr. Goodman decided to probe further and asked: "If you had control over it, would you choose to die in the morning, afternoon, evening, or at night?"

"Makes no difference," K.M. immediately replied.

"Would you prefer to die in spring, summer, fall, or winter?"

"No preference."

Somewhat annoyed, K.M. wanted to know why anyone would consider such useless questions. When asked whether he considered his death an important event in his life, he responded, "Yes, probably one of the most important events." He admitted that he had preferred times and places for other major events in his life, but he had never thought along this line in terms of death. Further questioning made him uncomfortable, and when asked if he'd like to know the full set of circumstances surrounding his death, he said emphatically, "I don't want to know!" "K.M.'s mood had changed drastically," said Dr. Goodman. "He had become less verbal, his former enthusiasm had completely disappeared, and he said he felt depressed." Eventually he admitted that his earlier statement—that he had long ago accepted his death and never gave it a second thought—was not fully true. He realized that he had never really accepted the idea of death, and for years he had repressed thinking about it. Death was often the subject of his dreams, and he now realized that at a subliminal level it apparently was always on his mind. Yes, he admitted, he had always been acutely aware of the fast passage of time, but no, he had not until now connected it directly with his suppressed thoughts of his own death.

Dr. Goodman advances a bold theme: "I believe that every accomplishment beyond the level of lower animals is a direct consequence of the challenge of death. The very essence of man rests on the knowledge of his mortality. From the building of permanent shelters, to the invention of means of transportation, to ever more distant places traversed in shorter and shorter times, to the conception and execution of the highest expressions in the arts, all this is founded on our knowledge of death. If we didn't know that our tomorrows were limited, the only conceivable struggle would be for immediate bodily comforts, as we witness it on the animal level."

Aside from death serving as a motivating factor in creativity, the death theme holds center stage in all forms of artistic creation: drama, dance, music, and the visual arts. In fact, from a careful study of history, one could make a case for artistic creativity reaching peaks in periods of the most open confrontation with one's mortality. "The lows," said Dr. Goodman, "exist in periods like our own, when denial of death becomes a major defense mechanism. Even the Middle Ages do not contradict this tenet; a period when creative endeavor was at an ebb while death was so rampant that people tried to repress the idea of it. The more death we see around us, the greater the need to deny it." Dr. Goodman is not alone in her conviction that if we force ourselves to confront the inevitability of our own death, it could have the effect of releasing untapped creative potentials and make every moment of our remaining life more precious.

The people who confront their own death most fully, of course, are those revived from clinical death. It has profound effects on their lives, and it should not be surprising that those who are influenced most strongly are the people who are convinced that while out of their body they meet their maker. Some of their stories are deeply religious. We will study three in particular.

In February 1970, Catherine Hayward, a California housewife and mother, was informed by her doctors that she had Hodgkin's disease—a usually fatal enlargement and inflammation of the lymph glands and the spleen. After a brief remission, the disease returned in March 1974, and Catherine felt certain that she was going to die: "I knew that it was only a question of time at that point. The children had already gone to live with their father. It was 10:00 P.M., June 30, 1974. I picked up the phone and called Ann, my dearest friend."

Ann arrived, and for several hours Catherine spoke

bravely about dying. Ann noticed her friend progressively weakening and insisted on taking her to the hospital. Catherine continued:

"After leaving my home, the last thing I remember is walking through the hospital door to the emergency room. When I awoke I was in the intensive care unit. Ann was there. There were wires and tubes attached to me. I was beginning to feel afraid. I heard an alarm and I saw a nurse run toward my bed."

Catherine's heart stopped beating and she had an OBE. While some clinically dead patients are uncertain of the voice that speaks to them, Catherine was not:

"I saw Him—the person I knew to be God. I moved faster toward Him—threw myself into His arms—and at last felt safe and secure. I heard the words, 'You must go back,' even though His lips had not moved. His right hand moved as gracefully as a flower swaying in the breeze. His left hand held me. His words sounded so stern.

"Looking back now, I laugh at my response, because I acted like a pouting child: 'I don't want to go back. I want to stay here with You.' He said, 'You have always turned to Me, now you must learn to be a child. This is something you have not experienced. It is time to accept what you are due. I tell you this: it will be a happier lifetime— you will know love—and I will not leave you, for you are Mine.' "

Catherine awakened in excruciating pain to find oxygen tubes in her lungs. Two days later she was moved back to her room, btu she felt so angry with God that she was too depressed to eat or to speak with anyone. On the evening of the second day she was rushed back to the ICU.

"Again I was out of my body—and there He was. Looking Him in the eyes, I felt ashamed and was not exactly sure why. After all, I had gotten what I wanted—to be with Him. He looked at me sadly and said. 'My compassion has brought you to Me again. I know you want to be with Me. If you do what I ask, you will come to Me and I will not leave you.' I nodded my head yes. He smiled—turned—and walked away.

"After that, I began breathing again. Each breath was easy and without pain. I knew that this was the beginning of a new life. I began to get my strength back."

Soon after, Catherine left the hospital and today she is a healthy, active woman, more religious and profoundly compassionate because of her experience. Miraculously, all traces of her disease are gone, and she has devoted herself to working with dying patients in several hospitals. One of her own doctors commented, "I have worked with people many times to get them to accept their death; but this was the first time I have ever had to get someone to accept life."

Many scientists are embarrassed or put off by the religious aspects of some death encounters. They are willing, even eager, to listen to tales of tunnels, lights, music, and the like—innocuous, "symbolic" things— but frown at or simply ignore statements to the effect that the person saw or spoke to God. We interviewed one researcher who said this about a patient's death encounter: "Her story would have been much more believable if she'd left out all that jibberish about religion and God." Another scientist commented: "I buy those death experiences up to the point when they start bringing in religion." Such attitudes are all too common. But the religious aspects cannot, and should not, be ignored; they are a vital—if not the most important—part of the death encounter.

We have found that sometimes a person strikes a bargain with God and a career is made on the other side. Dr. Norman Sand, a cardiologist, was in an automobile accident and was rushed to the emergency room of a city hospital in Portland, Oregon. Around one o'clock the next morning, following surgery, Dr. Sand was pronounced dead. He traveled out of his body and was in the presence of magnificent lights, drenched in "calm music," and having a discussion with a universal force:

"I would have to refer to the being as a universal force. I suppose if there had been a physical form there I would make use of the term God, but because of the absence of any form, I really don't know what to call it, but I would say that there was a consciousness, a life force, a universal consciousness there, and that there was an exchange between us, a discussion around whether or not this was the time that I should die.

"I remember a couple of things. The sensation I had was stronger than words can express. It was like a tremendous amount of energy was being used to make the decision as to whether I should live or die. I was sixteen years old at the time and I remember talking about the fact that I felt that I had not had an opportunity to really do anything with my life, and I got into a bargaining contest, saying that if I were allowed to live I would dedicate my life to trying to improve the quality of life and to providing some service to my fellow creatures.

"We struck a bargain that I would live doing the things I had promised, and that I'd come back, or die, when I turned fifty. At sixteen, fifty seemed so far away. Now I have a little concern about what will happen when I turn fifty in a few years. I have no intention of making it a self-fulfilling prophecy, but I really am curious about what's going to happen on my fiftieth birthday."

Dr. Sand remembers seeing doctors preparing to put his body into a "green plastic bag," convinced that he was dead beyond reviving, when suddenly "spontaneous respiration occurred." He remained in a coma, but later, he remembers, he was aware of doctors periodically coming into his room with a "pin stuck through an eraser on a pencil," which they used to prick him and check for reflexes. He claimed that it seemed to require a tremendous amount of energy to come back to life, and, "I would say that my parents were probably putting forth a lot of energy in the direction of trying to hold on to me." Dr. Sand kept his part of the bargain and devoted his life to helping others. It remains to be seen if his good works will be rewarded with a stay of execution.

We spoke with another doctor, a psychiatrist, who had his own encounter with death, one in which he met his maker, and today he is convinced that he was personally shown an existence after this life. Dr. George Ritchie is now in his fifties, with a psychiatric practice in Charlottesville, Virginia. His story is exceptional in many ways. It occurred in 1943, and he wrote down the details shortly thereafter, more than two decades before thanatologists started to collect such experiences. Yet, Dr. Ritchie's story contains virtually every significant element of the clinical-death experiences collected by a variety of researchers; in fact, it was Dr. Ritchie's experience that first launched Dr. Raymond Moody on his investigation. Dr. Ritchie's clinical death is well documented by Army hospital records, and his experience was a powerfully religious one that changed his life and deeply affected the lives of people he has shared it with in his lectures.

At the Army hospital at Camp Barkeley, Texas, early in December 1943, young George Ritchie was recuperating from a serious chest infection. He was eager to leave the hospital so that he could enter medical school in Richmond, Virginia, as part of the Army's doctor-training program. In the early morning hours of December 20, his fever suddenly soared and he became delirious before he blacked out.

"When I opened my eyes, I was lying in a little room I had never seen before. A tiny light burned in a nearby lamp. For a while I lay there, trying to recall where I was. All of a sudden I sat bolt upright. The train! I'd miss the train to Richmond!

"I sprang out of bed and looked around the room for my uniform. Not on the bedrail. I stopped, staring. Someone was lying in the bed I had just left. I stepped closer in the dim light, then drew back. He was dead. The slack jaw and the gray skin were awful. Then I saw the ring, the Phi Gamma Delta fraternity ring I had worn for two years."

Terrified, but not fully realizing that the body in bed was his own, Ritchie ran into the hall and shouted at an orderly, only to find that he could not be heard. "The orderly ignored me, and a second later he passed the very spot where I stood as though I was not there." Ritchie passed through a closed door "like a ghost" and found himself "flying" toward Richmond, obsessed with beginning medical school.

"Suddenly one thing became clear to me: in some unimaginable way, I had lost my firmness of flesh. I was beginning to know, too, that the body on that bed was mine, unaccountably separated from me, and that I must get back and

145

rejoin it as fast as I could. Finding the base and the hospital was no problem. I seemed to be back there almost as soon as I thought of it."

Dashing from room to room, inspecting the figures of one sleeping soldier after another for the familiar fraternity ring, Ritchie frantically searched for his own body.

"At last I entered a little room with a single dim light. A sheet had been drawn over the figure on the bed, but the arms lay outside. On the left hand was the ring. I tried to draw back the sheet, but I could not seize it. I thought suddenly, 'This is death.' "

It was at that moment that Ritchie fully realized he was dead. He felt depressed—his dream of entering medical school was shattered. As he gazed down at his body, despairing, something attracted his attention.

"The room was beginning to fill with light. I say 'light' but there is no word in our language to describe a brilliance that intense. I must try to find words, however, because, incomprehensible as the experience was to my intellect, it has affected every moment of my life since.

"The light which entered that room was Christ: I knew because a thought was put deep within me, 'You are in the presence of the Son of God.' I have called Him 'light' for that room was flooded, pierced, illuminated by the most total compassion I have ever felt. It was a presence so comforting, so joyous and all-satisfying, that I wanted to lose myself forever in its wonder."

Ritchie's entire boyhood flashed before him and the light spoke, asking him, "What did you do with your time on earth?" He stammered and stuttered, explaining that he was too young to have done anything of significance, and the light responded gently, "No one is too young." Ritchie's feelings of guilt were interrupted by a new vision, one so extraordinary that in reading his account, it is worth remembering that he is an intelligent, experienced psychiatrist who has spent a lifetime separating illusion from reality.

"A new wave of light spread through the room and suddenly we were in another world. Or rather, I perceived a very different world occupying the same space. I followed Christ through ordinary streets and countrysides thronged with people. People with the unhappiest faces I ever have seen. I saw businessmen walking the corridors of the places where they had worked, trying vainly to get someone to listen to them. I saw a mother following a sixty-year-old—her son, I guessed—cautioning him, instructing him. He did not seem to be listening.

"Suddenly I was remembering myself, that very night, caring about nothing but getting to Richmond. Was it the same for these people? Had their hearts and minds been all concerned with earthly things, and now, having lost earth, were they still fixed hopelessly here? I wondered if this was hell. To care most when you are most powerless; this would be hell indeed.

"I was permitted to look at two more worlds that night—I cannot say 'spirit worlds' for they were too real, too solid. The second world, like the first, occupied this very surface of the earth, but it was a vastly different realm. Here was no absorption with earthly things, but—for want of a better word to sum it up—with truth.

"I saw sculptors and philosophers, composers and inventors. There were universities, libraries, and laboratories that surpass the wildest inventions of science fiction.

147

"Of the final world I had only a glimpse. I saw a city—but a city, if such a thing is conceivable, constructed of light. At that time I had not read the Book of Revelation, nor anything on the subject of life after death. But here was a city in which the walls, houses, and streets seemed to give off light, while moving among them were beings as blindingly bright as the One who stood beside me."

The next instant Ritchie found himself back in the Army hospital, in bed, in his body. Weeks passed before he was well enough to walk around, and all the while he was obsessed with the thought of sneaking a look at his medical records. When he did manage to slip unnoticed into the records office, he found that his chart read: "Pvt. George Ritchie, died December 20, 1943, double lobar pneumonia." Dr. Ritchie told us:

"Later, I talked to the doctor who had signed the report. He told me there was no doubt in his mind that I had been dead when he examined me, but that nine minutes later the soldier who had been assigned to prepare me for the morgue had come running to him to ask him to give me a shot of adrenaline. The doctor gave me a hypo of adrenaline directly into the heart muscle, all the while disbelieving what his own eyes were seeing. My return to life, he told me, without brain damage or other lasting effect, was the most baffling circumstance of his career."

The incident had a profound effect on young Ritchie. Not only did he complete medical school and specialize in psychiatry, but he also became a minister in his church. A few years ago Dr. Ritchie was asked to recount his experience for a group of physicians at the University of Virginia Medical School. In order to see whether any relevant details of the experience lay hidden in Dr. Ritchie's subconscious, another psychiatrist hypnotized Dr. Ritchie and took him back to the time of his brush with death. Suddenly the veins in Dr. Ritchie's neck bulged, his face flushed, and his blood pressure soared; he was going into congestive heart failure as he relived his death. The psychiatrist immediately awakened him. It was apparent to everyone present that Dr. Ritchie's death encounter was so indelibly etched in his mind that under hypnosis he was capable of fully recapturing it—psychologically and physiologically. That fact has made many doctors reluctant to further probe the minds of people who have survived clinical death. It is conceivable that the most remarkably long deaths—those experienced through hypothermia and cold-water drownings—contain tales that will never surface.

Hypothermia, or "nonthermic" death, offers the most dramatic returns from beyond. In freezing, body temperature drops eight to twelve degrees and a person can remain clinically dead for hours and be resuscitated without brain damage. The two longest deaths on record are those of Jean Jawbone, a twenty-year-old Canadian woman who was dead for four hours, and Edward (Ted) Milligan, a seventeen-year-old Canadian boy who was dead for almost two hours. The cases are medical marvels, but because they occurred in Canada they are not known to many researchers in the United States. This is a pity, because they just might contain the most spectacular OBE adventures and the most elaborate descriptions of an afterlife ever. If the stories can be retrieved.

In the early hours of January 8, 1977, Jean Jawbone was walking home from a party in freezing snow in her hometown of Winnipeg, Canada. Numbed by the cold and already slightly dizzy from consuming too much alcohol, she passed out in a lane behind William Avenue. At seven o'clock, Nestor Rusnak was taking out his garbage before going to work when he spotted Jean's body; to keep her warm he wrapped her in a one-foot piece of carpet from his basement. Due to a mixup in communications, the police did not arrive until 8:15 A.M. They found Jean alive and moaning, but when she arrived at General Centre Hospital at 8:45, her heart had stopped beating. Her body temperature was 26.3° C.—about eleven degrees below normal. She had no heartbeat, no pulse, no respiration, and her pupils were fully dilated. The liquor she had consumed that night had hastened the drop in her body temperature, as alcohol dilates the blood vessels at the skin surface and allows heat to escape faster.

During the four-hour resuscitation, a total of seven doctors, ten nurses, and several orderlies worked tirelessly on Jean. The staff first tried external cardiac massage—depressing the breastbone toward the spine and squeezing the heart. A tube was inserted into Jean's windpipe through her mouth and the staff applied manual ventilation with a breathing bag. For two hours they tried, unsuccessfully, to raise her body temperature significantly—a necessary procedure before heart movement can be resumed. They covered her with heating blankets and hot towels, and inserted a tube through her mouth into her stomach, pouring warm saline solution into it—a method called peritoneal dialysis. That worked. Slowly, Jean's body temperature rose five degrees. It took more than another hour to get her heart started. After her body was sufficiently warm, a defibrillator was used to give her heart the electrical jolt that established a regular heartbeat.

By eleven o'clock that night Jean had regained consciousness, and after a period of grogginess she was able to talk. One physician on the staff, familiar with the imagery of death encounters, questioned Jean, but she appeared to have total amnesia; actually, retrograde amnesia extending back to the previous night's party. Dr. Gerald Bristow, a member of the resuscitation team, told us that Jean's brain was completely without oxygen for half an hour, yet she showed no signs of brain damage; her low body temperature slowed her metabolism so much that her brain required considerably less oxygen than normal. This appears to be responsible for the amnesia. The doctors we spoke with believe that somewhere in Jean's memory bank are the events of the party and her walk home. They believe that if those events could be brought to the surface, with them might come recall of the longest death encounter on record. For some reason, Jean has been very uncooperative, refusing to discuss her accident with her doctors. While some doctors caution that hypnotic regression could be dangerous for Jean because her death was so emotionally and physiologically traumatic, others believe that gradual regression, coupled with specific instructions that Jean's memory alone recall the latest events and that her body not react to them, might produce significant results. Jean, however, does not want recall, and for the time being, at least, is satisfied with her amnesia. Perhaps it is because there is something there that she does not wish to remember.

On the other hand, Ted Milligan, another hypothermia victim, was willing to submit to hypnosis. On the morning of January 31, 1976, Ted and other members of St. John's Cathedral School in Selkirk, Canada, were taking part in a compulsory twenty-five-mile five-hour snowshoe expedition. It was a mild Saturday and the boys were dressed lightly. About 4:00 P.M., three hours after the trip began, the temperature dropped suddenly to -15° C. and a strong wind rose. The boys were walking in groups of four, heading north into the town of Selkirk, when Ted became drowsy and tripped over his snowshoes. His companions thought he was just tired, but about a mile and a half from the school Ted collapsed.

One boy stayed with him while two others ran ahead

to find a snowmobile and call an ambulance. Meanwhile, another four students coming up from behind put Ted on their snowshoes and carried him half a mile. At this point the snowmobile arrived, and Dr. Gerald Bristow, the physician credited with reviving Ted, estimates that it took about an hour and a half to get Ted back to school.

Once at school, Ted was stripped of his clothes and put to bed under blankets; his skin was so cold that two other boys got into bed with him to try to warm him up. He was unconscious. The school nurse was the first person to check Ted's pulse and she realized that he was dead. She began mouth-to-mouth resuscitation and others began to massage his heart until an ambulance arrived.

At the Selkirk General Hospital, Ted's body temperature was recorded on arrival as 25° C., (77° F.). Normal body temperature is 37° C. (or 98.6 F.). It took five doctors and ten nurses two hours before Ted's heart responded. He was covered with hot towels (resulting in slight burns on his thighs) and given warm tap-water enemas, and drugs were injected directly into his heart. A tube inserted into his windpipe provided him with oxygen. Slowly his body temperature returned to normal, and although his heart did not beat for more than an hour and a half, and his brain was completely without oxygen for fifteen minutes, he suffered no brain damage. He did suffer retrograde and post-resuscitation amnesia, however, and could not remember what happened after the group had left the school for their hike, or the events for several hours after he had regained consciousness.

Ted's memory is slowly returning. When we spoke with him in the spring of 1977, he recalled the first part of his trip and some of the time he spent in the intensive care unit after being revived. Dr. Bristow believes that deep in Ted's subconscious might be a vivid tale of his encounter with death. Ted told us he was willing to undergo hypnosis to root out that tale, and his parents have tentatively given their consent. Before taking any risk, however, his doctors are waiting to see if more recall occurs naturally with the passage of time.

Ted did say this about his experience:

"When I first woke up, gained consciousness, the nurses told me my heart had stopped for a record time and that I had frozen to death. I thought it was all a lot of bull. Then they convinced me, and I was shocked. Why me? I kept saying. I was always somewhat religious—we all attend Anglican Sunday-night sermons weekly at school—but the death experience made me more religious. If I had to die again, freezing would be the best way to go. I felt no pain, no agony, nothing at all."

Death by hypothermia is only one untapped area for possibly rich tales of a hereafter. Another is death by drowning in cold water. Brian Cunningham, an eighteen-year-old student from Jackson, Michigan, was trapped under the ice of a frozen pond for thirty-eight minutes. Rescuers pronounced him dead at the scene, but he was revived and two weeks later returned to college with no physical or mental damage. A physician also drowned in a lake near Ann Arbor, but after fifteen minutes of submersion, he too was revived, showing no mental impairment. These are but two of fifteen unique cases of "cold water drowning" that have led Dr. Martin J. Nemiroff, an assistant professor at the University of Michigan's Medical Center, to conclude that all persons pulled out of the water blue, breathless, and apparently dead are not necessarily dead, even if they have been under water for more than thirty minutes.

Dr. Nemiroff's conclusions—and his collection of successful resuscitations—contradict the old belief that a drowning victim is unlikely to survive after four or five minutes under water. This limit is based on the fact that the human brain suffers irreversible damage if it is deprived of oxygen for more than five minutes. But Dr. Nemiroff has shown that in the fifteen cases he studied, all in water below seventy degrees Fahrenheit, eleven victims were revived without brain damage or other ill effects. What saved the people, says Nemiroff, is the activation of an automatic response in mammals called the "mammalian diving reflex"—combined, of course, with the coldness of the water, which helped to lower their metabolism and thus decrease their oxygen requirements.

The diving reflex was first identified in seagoing mammals such as the whale and porpoise. The porpoise can, in an emergency, remain submerged without breathing for twenty minutes, the whale for up to two hours. The reflex slows the heartbeat and constricts the flow of blood to the skin, muscles, and tissues that are more resistent to oxygen-loss damage. At the same time, the remaining blood oxygen is directed to the heart and brain. The cold water reduces the oxygen need of tissues and further lengthens a survival time without external oxygen.

Dr. Nemiroff has shown that in drownings in Florida and Southern California, where water temperatures are around seventy degrees, five minutes is the limit for unimpaired survival. He found that the diving reflex is more apt to be effective in younger people, particularly children under three and a half years old. He attributes this to a protective fetal response carried over from the period of time a baby must breathe in a fluid environment. Most bodies of water in the northern half of the United States are generally below seventy degrees. It is frightening to think how many thousands of people have been pulled from water blue, breathless, and presumed dead, when they could easily have been awakened with just a little effort.

Would they have had a death encounter to relate? Victims of cold-water drownings suffer from amnesia much the same way hypothermia victims do, and for very similar reasons. However, Brian Cunningham, the college student who was dead for thirty-eight minutes, does have fragmentary recall of the moments preceeding his "blank out." The panic he initially experienced from being trapped beneath the ice vanished and was replaced with "feelings of peace and utter calm." Mental activity grew "hazy," and just before loosing awareness he recalls being engulfed in a "bright blue mist" that seemed to assure him that everything would turn out fine. No one yet has tried to hypnotize Brian, or any other cold-water-drowning victims, to see what stories might be hidden in their subconscious. Of course, it is possible that they actually did experience nothing, but, given the evidence from other near-death encounters, that seems unlikely in every case. If anything, in hypothermia and cold-water drowning the astral body has plenty of time to separate from the physical, to travel, to observe, to encounter bright lights and spirit entities, and to try to contact family and friends. We believe that a special effort should be made by qualified researchers to elicit death encounters in these potentially rich cases. It is an area too long overlooked.

PART III

9

Mini-Deaths in the Laboratory

The scientific method requires rigorous proof of any new phenomenon. The more unorthodox the phenomenon, the more rigorous the proof must be. This usually means devising a laboratory experiment that when repeated time and again, by any competent researcher, in any laboratory, in any part of the world, yields the same results. The scientific method is relatively easy to apply in the fields of thermodynamics, atomic physics, physical and organic chemistry, and in general throughout most of the physical sciences. Here, the elements under scrutiny don't have a will of their own; once external variables such as temperature, pressure, humidity, and the like are held constant, the phenomena manifest themselves in the same way again and again.

The psychological and behavioral sciences present an entirely different picture. Rats, rabbits, and monkeys can be temperamental. The best experimental protocol might crumble because on a particular day a pigeon is not hungry for a tasty reward, or a nasal infection has rendered a hamster unable to sniff his way through a maze. The ability to repeat the experiment over and over again, and to employ statistical methods, becomes essential to satisfy the requirements of the scientific method.

Psychological phenomena are even more capricious. For human beings' thoughts, reactions, and general behavior are more varied and less predictable than those of animals. We have a will, often recalcitrant and stubborn. This presents a problem in all the psychological sciences, and it is especially serious in parapsychology, where the very events under investigation are themselves subtle, fleeting, unconsciously triggered, and poorly understood by the subject as well as the researcher. Even the greatest patience and the best experimental protocol cannot always elicit paranormal results—and predictable ones at that.

Survival research is the most difficult of all areas to study. Death is a delicate subject to discuss even in the abstract; and how do you bring it into the laboratory to study? Some researchers, however, now think they have a way to do just that.

For centuries psychics have claimed that OBEs are mini-deaths. In the last few years much new evidence has emerged to support that claim. Some of it has come from people who can induce their own OBEs and, for various reasons, have also experienced clinical death. They are able to make comparisons between the two: there are many striking similarities, and some very important differences. (We should expect some differences, since the physiological aspects of an OBE are unlike those of clinical death.)

Psychic Ingo Swann, we have seen, finds his OBEs and his two brushes with death similar in that in all cases he was able to transcend physical distance. Merely wishing to be at a certain location was enough to transport him there; yet, he could travel there leisurely if he wished. Other people also report this, and add that the feelings of calm and peacefulness are the same. One noticeable difference, however, seems to be that for most people, clinical death possesses a religious dimension that OBEs lack. Why should this be so?

Some parapsychologists believe that in clinical death a person is much closer to permanent death and "further into the death experience." Consequently, his encounter has religious overtones and, on awakening, may profoundly affect his life. According to this argument, death is a gradual process in which tranquility, sensations of floating, and astral travel characterize the earliest stages, while dark tunnels, bright lights, voices, music, and spirits appear at a later stage. If this were not true, people who can induce their own OBEs would see too many heavenly sights and thus tempted not to return to their body. For if we, at will, could glimpse all the splendor that most clinical-death survivors report, we would probably spend most of our time trying to launch our astral bodies into orbit.

However, every rule in nature does have exceptions, and they are always worth special attention. Some people do have OBEs unrelated to accidental death, and they still have religious aspects. Cases vary in their spiritual intensity. One highly notable case, replete with afterlife overtones, occurred to Massachusetts housewife Claudette Kiely.

If a link can be drawn between voluntary OBEs and actual death encounters, Claudette's case does it. At 6:05 A.M. on September 11, 1961, Claudette Kiely had her third child, a girl, at the Providence Hospital in Holyoke, Massachusetts. She was weakly smiling when the doctor leaned over her and explained that there was a complication—the placenta was not separating from the uterus and she was loosing a tremendous amount of blood. Claudette recalled:

"I began to silently pray to St. Gerard, the patron saint of mothers. Then I heard the doctor

161

shout to the anesthetist, 'Put her out!' Before they clamped the mask over my face I said aloud, 'St. Gerard, help them please.'

"The pain was gone, and so too were the doctors and nurses. I was aware of floating, fully conscious, at the entrance of a dark tunnel. I didn't hesitate to go inside. That was when I first saw the light. I remember wondering how something so dazzling could be so pleasant to look at. Somehow I instinctively knew that I had to reach that light—then I'd be at complete peace. I guess I was about halfway there through the tunnel—it's hard to estimate in terms of our notion of distance —when I heard a voice. It was distinctly male. 'Claudette,' he said, 'go back.' His words were incredibly gentle and at the same time commanding. 'I don't want to,' I said. 'Please let me come to the light.'

" 'You must go back, Claudette.' There was great urgency in his voice, and, paradoxically, great softness. I knew he would not force me; the ultimate decision was mine. I continued to float, determined to get to the light, and finally he said, 'Claudette, what about your new baby?'

"For some reason, I had no recollection of the baby and said so. He quickly added, 'What about your sons, John and Gerard?' That made me stop dead in my tracks. John was only twenty-two months old and Gerard was only eleven months. I remember shouting, 'Please, please, help me get back.' "

Claudette awakened. She spent the next several hours in the intensive care unit, until the doctors were sure she would not hemorrhage again. Claudette later told her experience to her doctor, and mentioned events that had occurred in the delivery room while she had been unconscious; he turned pale and refused to discuss the case.

In 1961, when Claudette had this experience, nothing much had been written about death encounters. Her experience had been too vivid to dismiss as a mere hallucination, so for years she thought her case was unique. Nine years passed, and then something unusual happened. Claudette began to have spontaneous OBEs. They took her to some pretty strange places: a power plant, a small restaurant, and other unlikely spots. Soon, though, she learned to control her OBEs and bring them on by simple relaxation techniques. To assure herself that she was not hallucinating, she became part of Dr. Osis's "fly-in" experiments in 1973. On five different nights, at prespecified times, she projected her astral body from her bedroom in Granby, Massachusetts, to the third floor of the offices of the American Society for Psychical Research in New York City. Claudette turned out to be a good subject and identified several target objects.

On one evening, researcher Bonnie Peraskeri was in the target room standing near the table that contained the targets. Bonnie noticed a blue mist developing near the table. "The mist moved in a cloud around the table, almost the way a person might go around a table to check out the objects on it," Bonnie recalled. Then the mist drifted toward the fireplace where Bonnie was standing. She was too fascinated to be alarmed. As quickly as the blue cloud had materialized, it vanished. The mist had appeared at the very time Claudette was astrally projecting at home. The ASPR staff was particularly interested to learn that that night Claudette had done her astral exercise wearing a blue bathrobe.

Claudette can induce her OBEs and has experienced clinical death. She finds the two very similar. "For me," she said, "there is actually very little difference—

though every time I have an out-of-body experience it is not the same." During her OBEs she claims that she has met spirits, conversed with them, and been in the presence of a brilliant white light; and occasionally when she is out of her body, as happened during one of the fly-in tests, the male voice, which Claudette now believes is God, asks her, "Claudette, why are you doing this again?" She answers, "I feel this work [the fly-in experiments] will help religion and science grow closer together." She said, "The voice has never answered back. It has never told me to stop having OBEs."

We have looked at mostly anecdotal evidence that suggests that OBEs in their fullest, complete sense are mini-deaths. But there is stronger evidence—evidence that comes from solid laboratory experiments.

Spirit photography captures on film images supposedly of deceased persons. The chemistry of what takes place in the film emulsion is well understood. Photons (massless, weightless particles) are absorbed by crystals, transfer their energy to the emulsion, and initiate a chemical reaction that causes areas of brightness and darkness (or of various colors if colored film is used) that render the final picture. For this to happen, a spirit, or astral body, must emit some kind of energy compatible with the chemicals in the emulsion—otherwise the film would not react. Thus, researchers suspect that astral bodies must be composed of energy.

The voice phenomenon captures on magnetic tape sounds supposedly emitted by the deceased. Again, what is required to activate magnetic tape is well understood. In the "audio voice phenomenon" where a microphone is used to tape-record the voices, the mechanical diaphragm of the microphone must be set into vibration. When a person speaks normally into a microphone, the vibrations from his voice set up a series of compressions and rarefactions in the surrounding air, and it is these high and low air pressures that cause the diaphragm to vibrate, sending electrical impulses to the tape. Thus, researchers suspect that astral bodies must be able to physically disturb air particles with their voices—or with their thoughts.

Further, a clincally dead person who "sees" events at a distance—or even in the operating room or the vicinity of his accident—must somehow possess a visual-sense modality. Naturally, researchers suspect that astral bodies must also have some optical component.

In short, all the sensory phenomena we have examined in this book can occur only if a person's astral body—or a spirit—has "sensory" components: vision, hearing, and touch (smell and taste seem less frequently manifest). To assuage their suspicions about these sensory modalities, researchers have devised some highly ingenious experiments to test for the audible, visual, and tactile senses of etheric entities. Some of the best work indicates that spirits—or astral bodies—can best be detected through their sensory manifestations.

Stuart "Blue" Harary, a psychic of Egypto-Syrian-Jewish parentage, has been studied extensively by scientists. Blue can easily induce OBEs simply by relaxing and attempting to project his astral body to some predetermined location. Drs. Robert Morris and William Roll were curious to see if Blue's astral body was psychically detectable—not by some sort of electronic equipment, but by living creatures—in this case, animals. Dr. Morris, an animal behaviorist who recently left the Psychical Research Foundation in North Carolina to accept a post at the University of California at Santa Barbara as a full-time lecturer on parapsychology, devised a novel set of experiments. They were carried out by Danish-born Dr. Roll at the PRF. The premise of the work is quite simple and very original. Parapsychological literature is full of references to the psychical sensitivity of animals, especially cats, which have served as companions to witches and seers for centuries. Do animals, which must rely primarily on their acute senses for survival, have the ability to detect astral or spirit energy? Cats and snakes were chosen in one set of experiments.

A young kitten was given to Blue. He raised it for a while, fed it, and attempted to develop a genuine rapport with the cat so that it was well aware of who he was. In the experiment, Blue's pet kitten was placed on an activity board that was shaped like a shuffle board and marked off into many squares; they determined the cat's activity by counting how many squares it moved during the experiment. Comparisons were to be made between the cat's movements when Blue was undergoing an astral projection into the box containing the checkerboard and when Blue was not projecting. The experiment worked beautifully. During control periods (when Blue was not projecting), the cat rushed about and vocalized profusely. However, when Blue was "present," the cat became very passive and did not vocalize; during these periods the cat behaved exactly as it did in Blue's physical presence. The statistical difference between the activity of the kitten during the control times and the experimental times yielded odds 100 to 1 that the result was due to chance.

Since the cat seemed to prefer different sections of the box at different times when Blue was projecting, the PRF scientists thought had the cat might actually localize Blue's presence. A new experiment was devised. The cat was placed in a large room and its behavior was monitored by closed-circuit TV cameras. Blue, in another room, had to project to randomly selected sections of the target room. Hopefully, the cat would go to the corner of the room where Blue astrally positioned himself. Mild results were obtained. At times the cat did go to the exact location that Blue was in. However, a surprise occurred. Dr. John Hartwell, the psychophysiologist monitoring the test, began having weird impressions as to where and when Blue was present. In fact, Dr. Hartwell became very successful at "guessing" when Blue was present. Once he not only correctly determined that Blue was present but actually saw his apparition over the monitor.

Psychophysiological readings were also taken of Blue during his projections; they showed differences in respiration, an increase in heartrate, a decrease in skin electrical potential, and an increase in blood pulse volume, but little brainwave change.

If Blue could have a calming effect on his kitten with the presence of his astral body, what would happen, the scientists wondered, if he projected himself into a glass terrarium housing a snake? Blue and Dr. Morris set up in one building; the snake was in another building with psychical researcher Dr. Scott Rogo, who was to monitor the snake's behavior. Dr. Rogo, of course, had no idea at what time Blue would attempt projection. At one point the snake made some pretty violent moves (having been motionless prior to this). It quickly ascended the side of the glass, bit and gnawed at it, then came back to the ground and remained noticeably excited. When notes and times were compared, it was found that the snake's strange behavior correlated perfectly with Blue's projection into the terrarium.

Dr. Rogo said, "The research with Blue Harary is probably the finest we have so far that links the out-of-body experience to the theory that during the experience something actually leaves the body. Blue's ability to affect animal behavior, the detection and even visual sightings of him, are all very consistent with the interpretation that he is physically present at a distant location during the out-of-body experience."

We have found that many people who openly balk at the thought that one person can see another person's astral presence readily accept the evidence that an animal can detect something as insubstantial as a spirit. It is a revealing commentary on our evaluation of our own potentials, and it might be just such a negative attitude that prevents many people from having paranormal experiences.

In 1975 psychic Ingo Swann took part in Dr. William Roll's experiments to see how clearly an astral body can hear at a distance. Swann remained in his apartment in New York and projected himself to a laboratory in North Carolina where Dr. Roll played various types of music: Latin beats, popular songs, ballads and classicals. Swann scored one hundred percent, guessing every musical number just as though he were physically present. The same experiment was tried with Blue stationed a quarter of a mile from the laboratory. He projected himself into the room, and correctly identified much of the music upon returning to his body. One psychologist familiar with the experiments thinks that the silver cord connecting the astral and physical bodies serves as a sort of communications link that transmits sensory information from the astral body to the physical brain, where it is perceived and interpreted.

Recently, more evidence has accumulated to show that the astral body is an entity unto itself, giving more credence to the belief in survival after death. Alex Tanous, the psychic who was Dr. Osis's star subject in the fly-in experiments, also gave a stellar demonstration in some in-house laboratory work. To determine if there is a real difference between clairvoyant perception and astral travel—a problem that has plagued researchers for decades—Dr. Osis worked with several physicists to come up with an "optical-image device." This is a structure about two feet on each side, containing a rotating disc divided into four quadrants, each of a different color. On one of these quadrants a small picture of an object (for example, an image of a chalice) is optically projected. Each time the switch is thrown, one out of five possible target images is randomly selected and becomes visible on one quadrant of the disc; the quadrant and its color are also randomly selected. The trick of the device is that an image and a colored quadrant can only be seen by looking through a small window in front of the device. Dr. Osis reasoned that if a psychic in another room used clairvoyant perception to view the device, he would make "wide sweeps" of it and see all four colors, and never see the target image since it is an optical illusion visible only by looking through the front portal.

Tanous was able to see both the correct color and the image projected. Dr. Osis had to conclude that Tanous's astral body was standing right in front of the portal, peering in (where Tanous said he was). On one try Tanous reported that he saw nothing but blackness, and when Dr. Osis's assistant checked, he found that the bulb in the box had burned out. Another time Tanous claimed that the optical device was too high, that he couldn't get up high enough to peer into it. A staff member put a small platform in front of the portal. The next time Tanous projected to the box, he saw its contents.

One of the most difficult sensory aspects of the astral body to study is its tactile sense. Psychics and some ordinary people claim that they have felt a "cool breath" against their cheek when trying to communicate with the deceased, and this occasionally occurs to people trying to take spirit photographs or to record voices on tape. Some psychics claim that they have actually been touched by spirits. And in poltergeist cases, physical objects lift into the air and move about a room. All this suggests that the astral body has psychokinetic ability too.

To investigate the extent of this hypothesis, the staff of the American Society for Psychical Research designed a "diving pool." It is an enclosed, opaque, electrically shielded space inside which an object is very delicately suspended on a string; a sensitive electronic instrument registers the slightest movement. Most people who had had OBEs failed to move the object on the string, but Tanous was able to slightly disturb the string when a feather was attached to it. Pat Price, another psychic from California, a former Los Angeles police chief who died in 1976, was so successful diving into the pool that he caused the recording pen to jump wildly on its graph. In another experiment, a fine talcum powder was spread over a black surface in the diving pool and Tanous had to astrally blow the talc. His success was too small to be statistically significant.

From all the work thus far, it seems that it is relatively easy for an astral body to see events and hear sounds, but considerably harder for it to move objects. Considering the etheric nature of an astral body and the physical mass of even a feather or talc, perhaps this is not at all mysterious. This laboratory evidence is in perfect accord with the reports of people who have experienced clinical death. They seem to have no difficulty seeing people, places and events, and hearing sounds, but those who try to physically touch a family member or knock over an object to get a person's attention find the task virtually impossible.

10

An Invitation
to Suicide?

"Before I started working with dying patients, I did not believe in life after death. I now believe in it beyond a shadow of a doubt." When Dr. Elizabeth Kubler-Ross made that statement in 1974 she shocked the scientific community and especially her psychiatrist colleagues. For years she had been acknowledged as the world authority on all "dimensions of death and dying." That meant careful studying of the emotional aspects of death and how they affect the patient and his family. It also meant recounting the stories told by dying and revived patients. Accepting those stories as proof of an afterlife was another matter entirely.

Surprisingly, several members of the religious community attacked her statement too. "Kubler-Ross's certainty must be a welcome boost to the feeble faith of many Christians," said one clergyman, "but it does not seem to work that way for me." The Reverend Robert M. Herhold, pastor of Resurrection Lutheran Church in San Bruno, California, thought that Dr. Kubler-Ross had gone too far. He retorted: "Life after

171

death is, by definition, beyond the range of scientific research; it is in the realm of the extrasensory, not the sensory. If life after death could be empirically verified 'beyond a shadow of a doubt,' then there would seem to be little need for faith." Another clergyman argued that "one does not need Easter if the soul is recycled, if it goes on living other lives." The critics seemed most alarmed at the preposterous prospect that if people everywhere were sold on the belief that science had proved there was an afterlife, there would remain little for religions to do.

A more predictable cry of criticism rose from psychiatrists, and in the last few years this has extended to the work of all researchers who collect and try to interpret reports of death encounters. Principally, the criticism centers on the possibility that the experiences of revived people are merely hallucinations, and one of the main critics is Dr. Russell Noyes, Jr., psychiatrist at the University of Iowa Medical School. Dr. Noyes has studied 114 cases of individuals revived from near-death encounters, and we have considered his breakdown of dying as a play in three acts, but he does not find death-encounter evidence to be even suggestive of an afterlife.

Dr. Noyes observed that the OBEs related by victims of accidents and death encounters "might be a basic adaptive pattern of the nervous system." He views this as "depersonalization," not astral flight. "Depersonalization appears to be an almost universal reaction to life-threatening danger," he said. The sudden release of pain that many people report, and the accompanying feelings of peace and calm, Dr. Noyes says, might be "an emergency mechanism, a sort of reflex reaction" so we don't have to suffer. Concerning the tales that seem to indicate survival, Dr. Noyes sides with Freud, who felt that the subconscious cannot contemplate its own demise, and that when confronted with inevitable

172

death it conjures pleasant, reassuring fantasies. Said Dr. Noyes, "Our own death is indeed unimaginable, so we perceive that we really survive as spectators. Thus, in the face of mortal danger, we find individuals becoming observers, effectively removing themselves from danger." Dr. Noyes sees the religious overtones of many death tales as hallucinations anchored to our religious beliefs. These views are shared by virtually all the scientific-minded critics.

These seem to be impressive arguments, rational and grounded in solid psychiatric and medical theories. However, we must realize that they are valid arguments against only one kind of evidence of survival: Death Encounters of the First Kind, the purely subjective experiences that lend themselves to scientific curiosity but in no way lend themselves to scientific proof. Unfortunately, Death Encounters of the First Kind have been the ones most publicized; they are the easiest to collect and perhaps the most abundant. But evidence of the Second, Third, and Fourth Kinds shatters the critics' arguments that the death OBE is a hallucination. When events nearby or at a distance are perceived by a person with no heartbeat, no brainwave activity—an unconscious individual—and when those events are later verified as fact, then the critics' complaints crumble. When one person senses in his gut that a family member or loved one is in grave danger, or possibly has died, and at that very moment the person in question has been involved in a major trauma, then the critics must find new arguments. And when a person sees, hears, or feels paranormal sensations—verifiable ones—then the critics should adopt an open mind and seriously ask how such things are possible. Can consciousness really separate itself from the body? Is survival a reality? Perhaps we will find this to be true, once researchers systematically study death encounters of the higher kinds.

Another, perhaps more valid criticism has been leveled against the tales from the dead. Virtually all such stories tell of peaceful and calm feelings; majestic panoramas; celestial music; luminous, radiant beings; meetings with deceased loved ones—all highly pleasant and desirable elements. Might such glowing tales of death actually encourage some people to commit suicide? As one psychiatrist put it, "Many emotionally disturbed or severely depressed people are deterred from taking their own life because they have no guarantee what lies beyond. If they were convinced that science had proved the existence of a wonderful hereafter, it could be just the thing to make them plunge the knife or swallow the pills."

Dr. Robert Kastenbaum, professor of psychology at the University of Massachusetts, believes this could easily happen—if it has not occurred already—and he thinks that in the long run, afterlife research will not comfort people but may eventually produce more suffering and pain in the here and now. Just when society is beginning to understand the emotional and physical distress of the terminally ill person, says Dr. Kastenbaum, we turn around and argue that dying is, in the end, a blissful experience. "The view that 'all's well that ends well'" assumes that everybody passes through a definitive moment of death," Dr. Kastenbaum said. "This is a questionable concept, not very well supported by clinical experience."

Other critics argue that we only have the stories of the people who have come back from clinical death: what about the millions upon millions more who made a permanent, one-way journey? Were their trips blissful? Did they have a chance to come back, but declined in favor of a more serene existence? Or did some of them experience horrors and suffering in the biblical tradition of hell? We just don't know. And we don't know why only about fifteen percent of the people revived from clinical death report awareness of an experience; the majority report nothing. "The close call or the temporary death may be quite distinct from the one-way passage from life," said Dr. Kastenbaum.

Other critics of the "happy death" experience emphasize the negative aspects. Some of their arguments are valid, but others are shot through with holes. They point to people in respiratory failure—choking on a bone, seized by an acute episode of emphysema, undergoing the terror of a massive drug side-effect—and rightfully say that these people feel as though they are in direct hand-to-hand combat with a very fearful death. Typically, these critics point to the pages of history that relate the dreadful events of premature burial: bodies exhumed with fistfuls of hair that had been yanked out in desperation, faces frozen in expressions of hellish horror, the walls of wooden coffins etched with clawing strokes to escape. But on a more careful look we realize that this criticism of the "happy death" hypothesis is invalid. Remember Dr. Russell Noyes's three stages of death: Resistance, Review of Life, and Transcendence. The horrors of premature burial, the agony suffered in an automobile accident or a fire, the despairing fright when a parachute refuses to open—these all belong to the Resistance stage of dying, Act 1, in which the human ego is actor and tries desperately to cling to life. When thanatologists speak of the peaceful aspects of death, the "happy death," they mean the final stage, Transcendence. A great deal of suffering and fright often does precede this stage, but the final curtain eventually does rise on Act 3.

Dr. Kastenbaum has searched for cases of genuine negative death experiences. He tells of a nurse who was involved in a car accident and arrived at a hospital in a traumatized state that rendered her paralyzed and mute, yet she could hear the sounds and voices around her. Dr. Kastenbaum recounted:

" 'This one is gone,' a voice was saying, 'let's get to one of the others next.' The nurse realized that *she* was the one who had just been dismissed as dead. Her response? 'I became furious—just plain furious! No way was I going to stay dead for them.' She determined to cross the invisible threshold between death and life. Summoning all her will power, she at last was able to attract medical attention with slight bodily movements and faint sounds. 'In my mind, I kept shouting, 'I'm not dead yet, you bastards!' I'm not sure if those came across to them, but some sounds did get out, and I wouldn't stop talking and moving until I had convinced them I wasn't DOA [dead on arrival].' "

Dr. Kastenbaum has used this tale to make his point that "the experience of this woman was much different from the type of account offered by Drs. Kubler-Ross and Moody. She was 'dead enough' to be taken for a nonsurvivor and passed over during the critical treatment-or-nontreatment period. Yet she did not flash above the situation, looking down in wonderment and bliss. She did not protest the efforts made to revive her or feel that a dream of celestial serenity had been destroyed by overzealous medical personnel. This woman wanted to live, and she did all in her power to summon the resources of a severely traumatized pronouncement of death as a stimulus for her recovery."

This case in no way challenges the "happy death" hypothesis or the validity of OBEs. The traumatized nurse suffered what is called a *social death* where a person is regarded by others as dead, however contrary the biological facts of the situation might be. The nurse's experience was clearly one of resistance. In searching for evidence that might disprove the "happy death" hypothesis, researchers must be careful to distinguish among the different stages of dying. Further, the fact that many people experience a brief period of transcendence moments before dying will never result in doctors and nurses ignoring the long-term needs of terminally ill patients. The idea that life ends with a moment of bliss will never affect the way in which society views the treatment of the chronically sick, slowly dying patient.

One real criticism of spreading "happy death" tales remains: the stories of a blissful death might encourage people to commit suicide. This being a likely possibility, it would be helpful to know if death by suicide offers the same experience as normal or clinical death. If the experiences are the same, for some people suicide might look like an easy escape from their problems. On the other hand, if a normal or clinical death provides a peaceful exit, while death by one's own hand results in a hellish journey, then suicide would not appear so inviting.

Unfortunately, the little evidence we have is conflicting. Many religions have severe admonitions against suicide, the most notable exception being certain Eastern sects that permit death by self-immolation and starvation in order to protest certain moral or social injustices. The punishments for suicide vary from eternal damnation in a fiery hell, to isolation in a realm of icy snow and blistering winds, to reincarnation in the form of an animal. None, obviously, is pleasant, and all are calculated to strongly dissuade taking one's own life.

Present-day knowledge of mental disorders has changed the traditional picture of suicide. Many religions concede that a person pushed to the extreme of taking his own life is by definition mentally unbalanced and therefore not responsible for his actions; he cannot be damned to an eternity below. It is a humane argument and comforting for relatives of a suicide victim.

On this ambiguous issue of the nature of the death experience through suicide we do have one firm fact: throughout the literature on death encounters, all those who have come back clearly reject suicide as a means of returning to the other side. Whether they came back because their doctors had revived them or because of a sense of duty to their family, they felt strongly that suicide was taboo, a forbidden way to obtain a repeat performance.

Some people who come back claim that in their out-of-body state they gleaned information that suicide was a despicable act punishable by severe penalties. One man who died told Dr. Raymond Moody:

"[While I was over there] I got the feeling that two things it would be completely forbidden for me to do would be to kill myself or to kill another person. . . . If I were to commit suicide I would be throwing God's gift back in his face. . . . Killing somebody else would be interfering with God's purpose for that individual."

A woman who was revived after taking a lethal dose of sleeping pills said:

"I was strangely conscious all the while [they worked on me] and very aware that what I had done was wrong. Not just by society's standards, but higher ones. I was so sure of this that I wanted desperately to get back into my body and live."

Dr. Moody is one of the few researchers who has considered the suicide angle and even his work in this area is sketchy, based on a few cases. However, Dr. Moody concludes that if there is any distinction between death encounters by suicide and by other causes it is this: natural death is characterized by feelings of peacefulness and a sense of "this is right, this is my ultimate destiny," whereas suicides are characterized by disturbed feelings, a sense of unrest, and a very definite intimation that "this is wrong, I must go back and wait for death." That information, scant as it is, is all we have to go on at the moment. Yet, it might be enough to dissuade some people from attempting to get into the hereafter before it is their time.

11

Life Before Life

If you hypnotize a person and gradually take him back to age five, he will speak as he did then. If you ask him to draw, he will execute the same bold, lopsided lines that he did in kindergarten. It's an amazing phenomenon to watch, but it is not at all mysterious. For stored in our subconscious minds are memory traces of all the events and behavior patterns of our past. If you age-regress that person further, to infancy, say, and leave him alone for a while, he will wail the familiar sounds of a baby wanting attention. He can even be made to speak nonsensical baby talk and thrash his arms and legs in wild, erratic patterns.

Anyone who can be age-regressed that far can be guided back still further. Back before the time of his birth. In these cases, when questioned about what they are experiencing, about twenty percent of the people remain silent. About eighty percent give fluent answers, often in voices unlike their own, and often of events that are unknown to them. When asked who they are, they give names of who they were in another life. Some researchers insist that this is proof of reincarnation. Others strenuously disagree. "It's a fantasy life," said one New York psychiatrist, "remembered from a historical novel or a movie; someone the person sub-consciously fancies himself to be. Under hypnotic age regression he can comfortably assume that identity without it conflicting with his real personality." In theory, both pro and con arguments can be made very convincing, but in practice there are too many cases that cannot be easily dismissed as fantasy projections.

Extracting tales of past lives is only one use of hypnotic age regression; currently it is also being used to study birth and death experiences. Dr. Helen Wambach is a psychologist in Walnut Creek, California. She has been age-regressing patients for many years and investigating their stories of past lives. Her main concern, however, is the impressions people have of their birth and early infancy. "My work for the last ten years has shown that people can vividly recall their actual birth." She did not always believe that. According to modern science, an infant's brain is not sufficiently developed to record and remember such experiences—certainly not in detail. The optic nerve is not fully operative in newborns, so naturally Dr. Wambach was interested in reports of her patients "seeing" the delivery room at birth. Emerging from the womb, one patient reported: "I see two windows, two chairs, and a table at the end of the bed with a basket on top of the table, and big puffy feather beds." After collecting many similar cases Dr. Wambach began asking herself, "Was I supposed to take these stories as out-of-body experiences at birth, or just pure fantasy?" Current research in parapsychology helped her find the answer.

Prenatal infants and newborns spend more than twenty of their daily twenty-four hours in rapid eye movements (REMs), which are indicators of dreaming in children and adults. The standard medical explanation for prenatal and newborn REM activity is that the neurons of the eye are firing at random. But random behavior of an organ as precise as the eyes seems unfitting. Dr. Stanley Krippner of the Maimonides Medical Center in Brooklyn has suggested that the long REM periods are times when the fetus or newborn is in telepathic rapport with its mother. The baby's body is physically dependent on its mother's body, so why shouldn't its mind be equally dependent on its mother's mind? asks Dr. Krippner. He also feels that infants might be dreaming during some of their REM time, an idea that contradicts the current medical belief that infants cannot dream because they have no experiences to dream about. All this got Dr. Wambach wondering and launched her into some pathbreaking research.

Dr. Wambach now feels that fetuses and newborns dream about experiences from past lives. One subject under hypnosis said that she had been killed in a war and floated out of her body, and was drifting when suddenly she was drawn to a woman with a developing fetus in her womb. She immediately went into the fetus, pondered her war experiences, and felt secure and safe until the day she was born. Several of Dr. Wambach's patients report rebirth following death in a war, and this has led her to speculate that baby booms that inevitably follow war might represent an opportunity for those many souls whose lifetimes ended abruptly to return immediately to finish tasks left undone.

"You don't have to be in a car accident to experience what dying is like," said the Reverend James Diamond of the Episcopal Center at the University of Minnesota. "We have all died in past lives, and under hypnosis we can witness that experience." Working with a psychiatrist, Diamond has been using hypnotic age regression first to take a subject back to a past life, then to have him relive his death. Their subjects described dying in exactly the same terms as people who have been revived from clinical death. "We have corroborated the stories of clinically dead people from the opposite direction," said Diamond. His subjects have reported floating out of their body, entering a dark void, and passing into a tunnel with a bright light at the end; they hear music, see images of spirits surrounding them, and are at first frightened, then at utter peace with themselves and their surroundings. The only difference is that these people reached the light, whereas those revived from clinical death are always interrupted before getting to it.

Diamond and his colleague make a highly desirable team to investigate the death experience and what it implies about an afterlife. This blend of the spiritual and the scientific disciplines is something we will undoubtedly see more of in the future. Their subjects have ranged in age from nineteen to forty-four and the only criterion placed on them is that they be easily hypnotizable. Otherwise they are ordinary people. The psychiatrist hypnotizes a person and "maintains a life-line with the ego," while Diamond interrogates the person. Every session is tape-recorded. The team has not yet released any of their case studies but plans to to so soon in a scholarly paper. They claim that by reliving the death experience through hypnosis, and being instructed to remember it on awakening, a person no longer fears death. "This could be a very simple way to eliminate the fear of death from everyone's mind," said Diamond. By remembering death encounters, Diamond's subjects also awaken more religious, convinced that there is an afterlife and a God, and that they experienced both at least once in the past and will experience them again in the future.

This century has witnessed a great revival of the belief in reincarnation, and with it the idea of karma. Karma implies a completely moral universe and holds a person responsible for his every action in every lifetime. Karma decrees that every decision has its consequences, and that decisions made in a past life generate the consequences that comprise our present lot. No soul is a blank slate. The subjects of karma and reincarnation lie at the foundation of modern parapsychology, and psychiatrist Ian Stevenson of the University of Virginia is largely responsible for the current popularity and respectability of these subjects.

Dr. Stevenson's involvement began when he submitted the winning essay "Evidence for Survival from Claimed Memories of Former Incarnations" in 1960 in a competition in honor of William James, the pioneer of psychology. In this essay he neatly turned the tables on most thinking about survival. He said, "In mediumistic communications we have the problem of proving that someone clearly dead still lives. In evaluating apparent memories of former incarnations, the problems consist in judging whether someone clearly living once died. This may prove an easier task."

Dr. Stevenson accepted the task and went on to make a very careful analysis of more than sixteen hundred cases of alleged reincarnation and to publish many in the prestigious *Journal of Nervous and Mental Disease*. A twenty-eight-year-old Brazilian woman, Maria Januaria de Oliveiro, lying on her deathbed, spoke to her best friend at her side, Ida Lorenz, a schoolteacher: "I promise I will return again and be born as your daughter. At an age when I can speak, I shall relate many things of my present life, and you will recognize the truth." One month after the woman's death, Mrs. Lorenz found herself pregnant. While she carried the child she thought continually of her dying friend's prediction, and after she delivered a girl, named Marta, she carefully watched the child grow. At age two, Marta shocked her parents by mentioning precise details of her previous life as Maria Januaria de Oliveiro. Dr. Stevenson interviewed Marta in 1962 and again in 1972 and found that while growing up she had made 120 statements about her previous life that were verified. Marta accurately described her father from her earlier life; she recalled that she had given her godson two cows before he died; she identified one of Maria's former sweethearts; and she knew that Maria and her mother, Ida Lorenz, had once bought identical horse saddles on the same day.

Dr. Stevenson has also found reincarnation cases that offer unusually strong physical evidence. Victor Vincent, a Tlingit Indian, was visiting his niece, Mrs. Corliss Chotkin, in Sitka, Alaska, about a year before he died, when he alarmed her by announcing: "I'm coming back as your next son. Your son will have these scars." He then pulled up his shirt and showed her an operation scar on his back and another short, irregular scar on the right side of his nose. Eighteen months after his death, Mrs. Chotkin gave birth on December 15, 1947, to a baby boy who, even at birth, strongly resembled his uncle Victor—and, incredibly, bore birthmarks that were identical to his uncle's scars. When Corliss Jr. began to talk at the age of thirteen months, he declared his name was "Kahkody"—the tribal name of Victor Vincent. At age two, he recognized a woman on the street as Victor's stepdaughter, Susie, hugged her affectionately, and kept repeating: "My Susie, my Susie!" That same year he also recognized Victor's son, William, and cried out: "There is William, my son!" A year later he recognized Victor's widow, Rose, and as he grew older he related many detailed incidents from Victor's life. On one occasion Corliss Jr. correctly pointed out the exact room in the house where Victor and his wife used to sleep when they visited the Chotkins—before Corliss Jr. had been born.

All these are fascinating and well documented, but Dr. Stevenson's prize case involves a Lebanese boy. Dr.

Stevenson discovered the case himself and was with the boy when he was first taken to the village in which he seemed to have spent a previous life.

From about age three, Imad Elawar seemed to know things that nobody had ever taught him. He mentioned by name a number of friends that his parents did not know, and they dismissed them as fantasies until one day the child rushed up to a stranger in the street of their village, Kornayel, and hugged him. The puzzled man asked, "Do you know me?" and Imad replied, "Yes, you were my neighbor." The man lived fifteen miles away, across the mountains, in the village of Khriby. From that moment, Imad's parents began to take him seriously, and by the time Dr. Stevenson arrived in Kornayel, to investigate another case, they had concluded that Imad was once Mahmoud Bouhamzy, who had been married to Jamile and had been run over by a truck, had both legs broken, and later died as a result of his injuries. Dr. Stevenson made a list of everything the parents claimed, and as far as possible tried to separate this from what the boy had actually said. Then he and the five-year-old child went to Khriby together.

There is very little contact between the two villages, and when they arrived there, Dr. Stevenson discovered that Mahmoud Bouhamzy did indeed live there, but he was very much alive. However, he learned that one Said Bouhamzy had in fact died in the way the boy described and that this man's closest friend was his relative Ibrahim Bouhamzy, who had been greatly affected by his friend's death and who himself died later of tuberculosis. Ibrahim had never married, but he had had a mistress named Jamile and had been a neighbor of the man Imad had recognized in Kornayel. Dr. Stevenson investigated the house in which Ibrahim had lived and found sixteen correct references to things like a small yellow car, two sheds used as garages, and an unusual oil lamp.

186

Dr. Stevenson's notes show that Imad had not actually said that he had been the victim of the truck accident, but merely that he remembered one vividly. He had spoken fervently of Jamile, even comparing her favorably to his mother, but never claimed to have been married to her. The errors of inference made by Imad's parents serve in fact as an indication of their honesty and make it extremely unlikely that they built up the whole thing as a fraud, or that they were the unwitting channel by which Imad received his information about Khriby. On the basis of the facts of the case, it seems that the memories of Imad bear a relationship to the experiences of Ibrahim that cannot be accounted for by chance, fraud, or normal memory.

Dr. Stevenson said, "We have left as serious contenders to explain it either some kind of extrasensory perception plus personation (whereby information gained by ESP is molded into a dramatic personal form), possession (by a spirit entity, presumably that of Ibrahim), or reincarnation."

Dr. Stevenson's work sparked new interest in studying the question of survival after death, but even as late as 1970 there were still relatively few researchers willing to tackle the subject. Some parapsychologists sided with the attitude held by J. B. Rhine, the father of American parapsychology, that the survival issue is a bad risk, a stalemated issue that can never be resolved, and that survival research should be shelved indefinitely so that more-fruitful research may be carried out. Others such as psychologist Gardner Murphy and his followers consider the issue completely deadlocked—that no evidence can ever prove that man survives death, that it indeed lies outside the reaches of the scientific method. What has brought about a change in thinking on survival as a valid area of research is the thousands of reports of people revived from clinical death. The commonalities among their tales, and how they so closely relate to ancient Eastern teachings found in the *Tibetan Book of the Dead,* have fired new interest in the subject.

To appreciate the change in scientific perspective between then and now, consider this seventy-five-year-old tale well known to parapsychologists. F.G.'s sister died of cholera when eighteen years old. Nine years later, F.G. was on a trip to St. Joseph, Missouri, and was filling out some business reports one afternoon in his hotel room. Something caught his eye and as he turned around he saw the figure of his sister staring at him. He was surprised to see a large red scratch on her cheek. When F.G. returned home to St. Louis, he told this astonishing story to his parents. His mother almost collapsed in shock, admitting that after the girl's death she had accidentally scratched her face but had carefully concealed it with powder. No one knew of the scratch but the mother herself. This was no idle story, since the testimony of all the witnesses was collected before the report was published in 1903. But consider how scientifically unconvincing that story must have sounded in 1903, and how it sounds after today's research on OBEs and clinical death. Sensitive equipment has detected the astral body; astral bodies can move objects, hear music, and frighten animals; during clinical death, a person can still have full awareness, travel to distant locations, and pick up verifiable details; photographs and tapes suggest that the dead are within reach. And this is only a small portion of the modern evidence we have examined. We would have to admit that the tale of F.G., considered quite bizarre in its day, is tepid compared to the contemporary cases we have studied. We can only guess how our perspective will change over the next decade, once clinical-death tales of the higher kinds have been systematically collected and statistically analyzed.

Writing in the *Journal of Nervous and Mental Disease,* Dr. Stevenson recently concluded: "The evidence of human survival after death is strong enough to permit a belief in survival . . . certainly there is much evidence suggesting human survival after death." The editor of the journal, Dr. Eugene Brody, a professor of psychiatry at the University of Maryland, commented: "This is one of the few times that work of this kind has been published in a prestigious medical journal."

Belief in reincarnation brings with it some hardnosed questions about this life. If, for instance, one lived a debauched, violent, crime-ridden past life, karmic law says he must pay for his wickedness this time around. Or next. Sooner or later we all must pay. This means that in some way we all are making payments now. One middle-aged Virginia woman who abandoned her newborn baby in a former life in order to continue her carefree existence reports that her punishment now is that she and her husband must remain childless—medically she cannot have children. A man who suffers from impotency and has had no luck with years of psychotherapy went, at the coaxing of a friend, to a psychic for a past-life reading. Without knowing his specific problem, she told him that in a former life he had been a rapist. He came away resolved to his fate.

The punishment does not always so neatly fit the crime. A New Jersey man who learned through hypnotic age regression that he once was a murderer believes that his life-long streak of bad luck (he has broken his leg twice, been in three serious car accidents and a near-fatal boat collision, and has been laid off from his last two jobs) is how karmic-law justice has sentenced him. Such cases suggest that subconscious memories of past behaviors and traumas can physically and psychologically disrupt our present life. In other words, our past might be responsible for at least some of our present problems, neuroses, and mental blocks. If this is true, it could account for those psychological hangups that repeatedly resist conventional psychoanalysis and psychotherapy.

An increasing number of psychologists believe that this is the case, and a treatment called past-life therapy now claims to be curing thousands of men and women of problems rooted in former existences. Nancy Shiffrin, age thirty-three, a freelance writer in California, has always had trouble finishing books and articles. For years she believed that the problem was rooted in her childhood fear of failing at any task and disappointing her parents. Now she claims that her writer's block began in the seventeenth century. During a session with Morris Netherton, a Los Angeles past-life therapist, Nancy had a vision of herself as a woman on trial in America in 1677 for heresy and trying to hide an incriminating diary from her inquisitors. Three hundred years later she is still "hiding the book" as she says. Knowing the source of her problem has apparently cleared it up. She claimed: "I seem to have very little problem finishing things now, as if the pattern were erased."

What past-life therapy does is take the conventional Freudian idea that much adult behavior is unconsciously governed by early traumas and applies it to the concepts of reincarnation and karma. In this respect the treatment becomes more Jungian than Freudian. Past-life therapy has been widely practiced in Europe for about fifteen years, but Americans are just beginning to take it seriously. So far the results are impressive.

One young woman had a child delivered by cesarean section and for the next eleven years refused to have sex with her husband. Her complaint, which she repeatedly stated, was: "He's too big for me." Through past-life therapy the woman found that she had died in several former lives during brutal rapes; and several times she had died during pregnancy. In the particular incident that seemed to be at the root of her problem, she found herself in medieval England. She was fourteen and pregnant by an important nobleman who desperately needed an heir to his title. At a certain point during delivery it became clear to the midwife that it was necessary to choose between the mother's life and the baby's. "He's too big for her!" the midwife exclaimed, referring to the baby, and without a second thought the nobleman chose the baby's life over the mother's. The woman died hearing the words "He's too big for her," and that phrase was governing her sexual relationship with her husband; the cesarean section is what triggered the latent memory. With the past trauma unveiled, the woman was able to resume a healthy sexual relationship with her husband.

Not all past-life therapists use hypnosis. Dr. Morris Netherton merely has his patients lie on a couch and relax while he throws key words and phrases at them. The phrases, he explains, are direct quotes from past lives, which he gleans from the patient in an interview. With Nancy Shiffrin, for example, he recorded her family and medical history during a lengthy interview, but also pieced together a phrase from her various comments about her work: "Think nobody cares about me, only the book, I have to hide the book." Once Nancy was relaxed on the couch, Netherton tossed the phrase at her and immediately asked, "Now tell me what you see, hear, think, feel. Quickly—what is the first thing that comes to your mind?" Nancy saw nothing, blackness, and Netherton explained that the blackness was obscuring a past life; with that, she saw herself in a courtroom being tried for heresy in 1677. "I'm being questioned about my religious beliefs by a group of men. They try to convince me it's my immortal soul they're interested in. Yet, they insistently ask me about the location of a diary that would reveal my true feelings." Netherton asked, "What are you thinking as they question you?" and Nancy responded, "They don't care about me, all they want is the book!" He had her repeat that phrase over and over again. "What else are you thinking about?" he asked. "I've got to hide the book!" Again he had her repeat that key phrase until all emotion was gone from it; then the session ended. Nancy was cured.

Most patients who undergo past-life therapy wonder if they actually experience a past life or just a fantasy, a sort of hallucination. But belief in reincarnation is not essential to the success of past-life therapy. Indeed, the cure rate seems to be independent of a person's reincarnation beliefs. Skeptics report as many cures as do true believers. In this respect, past-life therapy seems no different from various other forms of psychotherapy that require the patient to take responsibility for behavior in this life. Past-life therapy seems to be an effective way to root out emotional traumas.

Some past-life therapists like Dr. Edith Fiore, author of *You Have Been Here Before*, use hypnosis exclusively. A homosexual who had an unhealthy dislike for women learned under hypnosis that in a past life he had been raised by two sadistic aunts who had brutally tortured him. The revelation did not make him heterosexual, but it did permit him to strike up warm relationships with women. At the Hypnosis Motivation Institute in Los Angeles, Evelyn Schiff has found that hypnosis greatly facilitates past-life recall.

She regressed one woman who chronically had difficulty learning and found that in a former life the woman's father had repeatedly slapped her around and called her "dummy." Since this revelation, the woman has had no difficulty learning.

Schiff has been even more innovative and used past-life therapy to treat physical ailments. She had a girl who habitually stumbled and often could not walk without support. Under hypnosis the girl reported that just when she was about to stumble and fall she felt a numbness in her ankle. Using that as a pivotal point, Schiff guided the girl back to the time that she first felt that sensation. She regressed to a life in a prison in which a heavy ball was chained to her leg, making it impossible for her to walk without stumbling. Now the girl has a perfectly normal walk.

Past-life therapy should not be thought of as a panacea; it has its drawbacks too. It is all too easy to blame present problems on what one believes to be past-life behavior. One attractive Philadelphia woman went to a local therapist already convinced that her intense inferiority complex was a leftover from a former life as a homely, uneducated girl. Under hypnosis she journeyed through six past lives, four as beautiful women and two as handsome men. When she later listened to a tape-recording of her experiences, she was convinced that she must have missed the homely incarnation. Three more sessions followed over the next month that did not support her belief; in fact, they continued to contradict it. The woman could not accept the fact that her present problem most likely stemmed from events in her present life and she refused to go back to the psychiatrist who had treated her for years.

The very nature of reincarnation makes it immune to proof by the scientific method. But more and more scientists are arguing that the scientific method, which for centuries has been ideal for handling objective realities, should be augmented to encompass subjective realities that are becoming increasingly central themes in modern psychology and quantum physics. At present, no one knows quite how to expand the scientific method without introducing logic loopholes. But one day it will be done, and then survival and reincarnation might be provable beyond a shadow of a doubt. In the meantime, favorable evidence continues to mount, and more and more scientists listen raptly to the tales of survivors of clinical death, while more and more skeptics become believers. Death Encounters of the First Kind will forever remain subjective experiences, but it is Death Encounters of the Second, Third, and Fourth Kinds that offer the strongest evidence yet of survival, reincarnation, and contact with the dead—evidence that is too awesome, and too important, to be ignored any longer.

Bibliography

Annas, George J. "Rights of the Terminally Ill Patient." *Journal of Nursing Administration* 4, March–April 1974, pp. 40–44.

Bander, Peter, *Voices From the Tapes.* N.Y.: Drake Publishing, 1973.

Becker, Ernest. *The Denial of Death.* N.Y.: Free Press, 1973.

Colen, B.D. *Karen Ann Quinlan, Dying in the Age of Eternal Life.* N.Y.: Nash Publishing, 1976.

Feifel, Herman. *New Meanings of Death.* N.Y.: McGraw Hill, 1977.

Fletcher, George. "Prolonging Life." *Washington Law Review* 42, 1967, pp. 999–1016.

Gaylin, Willard. "Harvesting the Dead." *Harper's Magazine,* Sept. 1974, pp. 23–30.

Gold, E. J. *American Book of the Dead.* San Francisco: And/Or Press, 1975.

Greeley, Andrew M. *The Sociology of the Paranormal.* Sage Research Papers, vol. 3. Beverly Hills: Sage Publications, 1975.

Grof, Stanislav, and Halifax, Joan. *The Human Encounter with Death.* N.Y.: Dutton, 1977.

Harvard Medical School, Ad Hoc Committee of the Harvard Medical School to Examine the Definition of Brain Death. "A Definition of Irreversible Coma."

Journal of the American Medical Association 205, 1968, pp. 337–40

Head, Joseph, and Cranston, S. L., *Reincarnation: The Phoenix Fire Mystery*. N.Y.: Julian Press/Crown, 1977.

Hendin, David. *Death as a Fact of Life*. N.Y.: W. W. Norton and Co., 1973.

Holck, Frederick, ed. *Death and Eastern Thought*. Nashville: Abingdon, 1974.

Kastenbaum, Robert, and Alsenberg, Ruth. *The Psychology of Death*. N.Y.: Springer, 1972.

Korein, Julius. "On Cerebral, Brain and Systemic Death." *Current Concepts of Cerebrovascular Disease: Stroke 8*, May–June 1973, pp. 9–14.

Kubler-Ross, Elizabeth. *On Death and Dying*. N.Y.: Macmillan, 1969.

Matson, A. *Afterlife: Reports from the Threshold of Death*. N.Y.: Harper and Row, 1975.

May, William. "Attitudes Toward the Newly Dead." *Hastings Center Studies* no. 1, 1973, pp. 3–13.

Monroe, Robert A, *Journeys Out of the Body*. N.Y.: Anchor/Doubleday, 1973.

Moody, Raymond A. *Life After Life*. Ga.: Mockingbird Books, 1976.

——. *Reflections on Life after Life*. N.Y.: Bantam, 1977.

Morison, Robert S. "Dying." *Scientific American* 229, Sept. 1973, pp. 55–62.

Osis, Karlis, and Haraldsson, Erlendur. *At The Hour of Death*. N.Y.: Avon, 1977.

Panati, Charles. *Supersenses: Our Potential For Parasensory Experience*. N.Y.: Anchor/Doubleday, 1976.

Rauscher, William V. *The Spiritual Frontier*. N.Y.: Doubleday, 1975.

Rogo, Scott D. *Parapsychology: A Century of Inquiry*. N.Y.: Taplinger, 1975.

Sadler, Alfred M. "Transplantation and the Law." *New*

England Journal of Medicine 282, 1970, pp. 717–23.

Stevenson, Ian. *Twenty Cases Suggestive of Reincarnation.* Charlottesville, Va.: University Press of Virginia, 1974.

Smith, Susy. *Voices of the Dead?* N.Y.: Signet, 1977.

Tanous, Alex. *Beyond Coincidence.* N.Y.: Doubleday, 1976.

Tibetan Book of the Dead. Berkeley, Ca.: Shambhala Publishing, Inc., 1975.

Veatch, Robert M. *Death, Dying and the Biological Revolution.* New Haven, Conn.: Yale University Press, 1976.

Walker, E.D. *Reincarnation, A Study of Forgotten Truth.* N.Y.: University Books, 1965.

Watson, Lyall. *The Romeo Error.* N.Y.: Doubleday, 1974.

Weidenfeld and Nicolson, eds. *Life After Death.* N.Y.: McGraw Hill, 1976.

Wheeler, David R. *Journey to the Other Side.* N.Y.: Grosset and Dunlap, 1976.

Worden, J. William, and Proctor William. *PDA— Personal Death Awareness.* Englewood Cliffs, N.J.: Prentice Hall, 1976.

ABOUT THE AUTHORS

ALAN LANDSBURG is a very successful film and television producer, heading up his own production company in Los Angeles. He was instrumental in bringing the von Däniken phenomenon to the attention of the American public through TV by producing the acclaimed "In Search Of Ancient Astronauts." He is also the author of a number of bestselling books including *The Outer Space Connection* and the *In Search Of* ... series.

CHARLES FIORE is a successful writer who now resides in New York City.

OTHER WORLDS
OTHER REALITIES

In fact and fiction, these extraordinary books bring the fascinating world of the supernatural down to earth from ancient astronauts and black magic to witchcraft, voodoo and mysticism these books look at other worlds and examine other realities.

☐ 12751	**LIMBO OF THE LOST—TODAY** by J. W. Spencer	**$2.25**
☐ 10688	**THE DEVIL'S TRIANGLE** by Richard Winer	**$1.75**
☐ 8376	**IN SEARCH OF ANCIENT MYSTERIES** by Alan and Sally Landsburg	**$1.50**
☐ 11137	**IN SEARCH OF MYTHS AND MONSTERS** by Alan Landsburg	**$1.95**
☐ 11989	**IN SEARCH OF ANCIENT GODS** by Erich Von Daniken	**$2.25**
☐ 11818	**VON DANIKEN'S PROOF** by Erich Von Daniken	**$2.25**
☐ 2968	**BIGFOOT** by Slate & Berry	**$1.50**
☐ 13005	**A COMPLETE GUIDE TO THE TAROT** by Eden Gray	**$2.25**
☐ 12528	**GODS FROM OUTER SPACE** by Erich Von Daniken	**$2.25**
☐ 11900	**BEYOND EARTH: MAN'S CONTACT WITH** UFO'S by Ralph Blum	**$1.95**

Buy them at your local bookstore or use this handy coupon for ordering:

Bantam Book Catalog

Here's your up-to-the-minute listing of over 1,400 titles by your favorite authors.

This illustrated, large format catalog gives a description of each title. For your convenience, it is divided into categories in fiction and non-fiction—gothics, science fiction, westerns, mysteries, cookbooks, mysticism and occult, biographies, history, family living, health, psychology, art.

So don't delay—take advantage of this special opportunity to increase your reading pleasure.

Just send us your name and address and 50¢ (to help defray postage and handling costs).